"A Florida Keys Novella"

The Keys
To
Montana

I0520434

Miki Bennett

This book is a work of fiction. Any references to historical events, real people, or real places are used fictitiously. Other names, characters, places, and events are products of the author's imagination, and any resemblance to actual events or places or persons, living or dead, is entirely coincidence.

Copyright © 2018 Miki Bennett

All rights reserved. Printed in the United States of America. No parts of this book may be used or reproduced in any manner whatsoever without the written permission of the author.

Second Edition

ISBN: 978-0-9988481-8-1

WannaDo Publishing, Charleston, South Carolina

This book is dedicated to all those that know love.
Never let it go.

1

"Are you sure that's all you need?" Charlie said, looking at the list in his hand then back to the man sitting behind the desk. "Shouldn't take too long. Be back a little after lunch."

"Sounds good," Seth said.

"Seth, are you sure you're okay?"

"Yeah. Why?"

"Just seem a bit distracted lately."

"I have a lot on my plate, but nothing I can't handle."

"Let me know if you need anything. Plus, you're invited to dinner again. Mary is making your favorite: beef pot pie."

"Thanks, Charlie and I'll take you up on that dinner invite," Seth said as he watched his right-hand man walk out of the office door.

Seth sat behind the large wooden desk, staring at the papers in front of him. They seemed to loom over him like one of the huge mountains outside his office window instead of the small stack they truly were. Ever since he had returned to the family's Montana ranch after visiting his father and Josie in the Florida Keys, he was restless. He had a hard time staying focused on anything related to the ranch which was completely out of character for him.

He loved Montana and felt blessed that his father thought him capable enough to run the large ranch he owned. Seth had taken to ranching like a fish to water. He had grown up in Seattle with his mother and stepfather but upon finding his real dad, it was as though Montana had called him back home where Seth felt he belonged.

Even the bitter cold winters hadn't fazed Seth. He embraced all the seasons that came with living here. He loved the mountains, hills, and valleys that surrounded him. But even though he had been home a little over two months from his three-week vacation to Florida, he couldn't help but think daily about the azure water, warm temperatures, and white, soft sand. The time spent out on his dad's boat, fishing or snorkeling. The wonderful food that greeted him on each Key he visited and the rich history of the islands. He loved every part of the Florida Keys.

But most of all, he couldn't forget the woman he had met in Key West: Ella. She was the tour guide on the glass-bottom boat Seth and his dad had gone on while visiting the city. Seth tried his best to concentrate on the sea life on the other side of the glass as he and others peered over the railing in the boat but it was next to impossible for him. He couldn't keep his eyes off Ella as she explained what ocean creatures they were viewing through the thick glass that separated them from the sea below.

At the end of the boat tour, Seth, who usually wasn't very spontaneous, found Ella as she was preparing for the next trip out to the reef. He asked her out, but she immediately said "no". But that didn't deter Seth. He came the next day, driving from Marathon, to see her again. And this time, she agreed to a quick drink after her last boat run, but it had to be fast. She also worked a waitressing job at night, and she had a shift that evening. Ella, who claimed that she had never called in sick since beginning either of her two jobs, made a call during the middle of their conversation and said she couldn't come in. Then, to Seth's surprise, she asked him to dinner.

The rest of the time he was in the Keys, though he had gone to spend time with his father and Josie, the woman his father had just been reunited with, was spent with Ella. He even stayed in a hotel in Key West for a few days just to be near her. Though she worked quite a bit, they were able to carve out time to be together and just talk, walk the busy city streets, or visit some of the wonderful restaurants in the tropical city. It was as if Seth had found his best friend, but he knew he wanted more. The problem was the ever-present fact that he would be heading back to Montana.

But since arriving back home, Ella was all he could think about. Yes, they texted back and forth every day. Their talks on the phone were at least three or four times per week, but Seth wanted to see her. To hold her in his arms again, like he had toward the end of his Florida Keys vacation. They had only kissed a few times right before he left, and he remembered every second of each one.

As he sat there thinking, he wished that he could jump on a plane this afternoon and be there tonight, just to see her again. Never had he felt this way about a woman, and fighting these feelings was beginning to feel useless. He had a large ranch to run, and taking off at the spur of the moment wasn't a luxury he could take at the moment.

"Hey, I need to ask you about one more thing," Charlie said as he came into Seth's office and took a seat only to be met by a blank stare from Seth.

"Hey, Boss, where you at?"

"What the hell are you talking about?" Seth said, looking suddenly puzzled.

"I don't know what happened in Florida, but you sure haven't been yourself since you got back."

"I'm fine."

"I'm guessing some girl has got a hold of you," Charlie said, laughing. "That's the only reason men look goofy, like you do right now."

"No, it's just much warmer there right now. This snow is early, and I'm thinking about how my dad is in flip-flops most of the year."

"Thought you liked the weather up here. Especially with the snowmobiles. And what about ice fishing? Can't beat that. No tropical island is that much fun."

"Believe me, Charlie, if you ever go down there, it will make you think twice about Montana," Seth said, knowing he was talking about the dark-haired girl he saw is his mind and not the warm weather.

"Nah, I'm where I belong. Have no interest in going south. Went to Disney World once, and that was enough of Florida for me," Charlie said, laughing. "Still have that picture with some Goofy hat my daughter made me wear. I need to get rid of it, but she has it hanging on her mirror still, even though we went when she was a little girl. Just glad the guys can't see it!"

"Next time you give me any grief over the barn, I'm calling your daughter for blackmail material," Seth laughed. Charlie was like a second father to Seth and someone whom he could trust completely with the ranch whenever he had to go out of town. Right now, Seth wanted to hand all of his responsibilities over to him and head down south to see a very special woman.

2

As the boat neared the dock, Ella looked out at the group of new passengers that were eager to get on the boat. She would have about an hour to get some lunch and sit for a few moments before heading back out to the reef.

Finding a shady spot right off Mallory Square, she brought out her lunch bag, where she had stashed two veggie wraps, some fruit, and ice-cold water. It was particularly hot today, and the cold lunch soothed her as she sat under the tree, watching tourists walk by. Ella quickly looked at her phone's time to make sure she wouldn't be late, and there was plenty of it to spare. But the main reason she had the phone available was to check her email and text messages for anything new. She scanned the mail, looking for Seth's name. Nothing yet today. Another check of her text messages, and his name did not appear there either.

Seth had been gone for quite a while now, and Ella finally admitted to herself that she was falling for the man. She had promised herself that this wouldn't happen till she was completely independent, not having to rely on anyone. She was almost through school, with only one online class left. Then she would get the Bachelor's Degree in Business she had worked so hard for these past years.

Her parents had practically begged her to stay in Miami and go to school there while she lived at home, but Ella wanted to be out on her own. A few of her friends had moved to Key West and loved every minute there. They would write to her or talk on the phone, and each time, Ella found herself wanting to move and be out on her own. But her parents had told her that if she did, she would find no help from them. The day she left Miami was so sad, even though she was only moving three hours away. Her mother cried, asking Ella to reconsider, but Ella knew in her heart that she was meant to come here.

She kept her parents updated with her progress, talking to her mother every week. Her father did not have much to say. As time passed, both her parents saw that she was capable and were now proud that their only daughter was making her way in the world and almost had her college degree. It had taken her longer than others, but Ella didn't care. They were proud of her, and she was proud of herself.

She did miss them, but Ella made sure to visit Miami every three or four months. Plus, her parents had visited her for the first time very recently, which was monumental for Ella. Once they saw how happy she was, they were content about their daughter being out on her own. Except they didn't like that she worked two jobs.

She remembered the first weekend trip she took to Key West, to visit her friends. Ella knew within just one day that she had found the city where she wanted to live. She and one of her friends from Miami moved there, finding jobs the day after they arrived. They shared an apartment and expenses. Everything seemed fine until her friend's mother became ill, and she had to go back to Miami. Ella found herself in the Keys by herself and with a large apartment lease. But instead of trying to find someone else to share it with, she took on two jobs to pay the bills.

It was while working those jobs that Ella made the decision to go back to school. She wanted a college degree. She was great with people and marketing and had even helped the boat charter company design their new ads and brochures. At the restaurant, Ella had helped the owner design the new menu and told him ways she thought he could advertise to bring more tourists in for their evening dinner. When her ideas were well-received, Ella knew the work she wanted to do. And having a degree behind her name would not only make her a more invaluable employee, it would boost her self-esteem.

Even though she should be working on her final class project during her lunch break, Ella would have rather seen a message from Seth. When he had left to go back to Montana, she thought her little romantic fling would be forgotten in a week. That definitely wasn't the case. It only took a few days of not seeing him, and Ella knew her heart was in trouble. For the first time, she had allowed someone into her life, over the boundaries she had self-imposed around herself when she came to Key West. She had been so focused, and she still was, but Ella couldn't quit thinking about Seth and the time they had spent together.

Seth was completely different from any other man she had met since coming to the city. He was most certainly cute, with his short, dark hair and deep, brown eyes. His chiseled jaw with just the right amount of stubble made Ella's heart beat just a little bit faster. To Ella, he was sexier than any man she had ever seen.

She remembered the first time they saw each other. It was a ride out to the reef. As the boat hovered still in the water, while Ella described the sea life they saw, she would glance at her captive audience and somehow always found Seth, catching him staring at her. But like men had done before in the past, this time it wasn't weird. It was flirty and Ella loved it.

Seth asked her out as soon as all the passengers were off the boat, and she said "no", citing that she was too busy, but it was more than that. She was trying to keep that promise she had made to herself. But the second time he asked, her intention to keep her life simple and uncomplicated suddenly went out the window, and Ella said she would go with him for a drink at the bar close by.

Ella had told him that it had to be a quick one since she was expected at work that evening. But their time together turned into a wonderful dinner. She tried to remain casual and aloof during the conversation, but she couldn't. Seth was beyond charming, and his sweet personality completely won her over before their entrées even arrived.

His stories of running a ranch in Montana fascinated her. She had never been farther north than Atlanta, and she had only ended up in the Georgia capital because her roommate at the time didn't want to go to a convention by herself. So, Ella had tagged along, visiting the city sights while her friend was working. But when Seth described where he was from, Ella was captivated. He described mountains that reach high toward the stars, bubbling cold-water streams, and snow in the winter that would pile in drifts taller than him. She had never seen snow before and couldn't imagine what it must be like to live in such a beautiful part of the country.

It only took a few days before Ella found herself wanting to see Seth whenever possible, and she wasn't disappointed. Well, maybe a few times, when he had plans with his father and Ella's former next-door neighbor, Josie. Other than that, they were together. Seth and Ella had practically visited every tourist site on the island, but then she also took Seth to some of the places that were the favorites of the locals.

It only took one week before Ella was totally smitten. But it wasn't till about four days before Seth was scheduled to go back home that he had kissed her. It was her one unusual night that she wasn't working her second job, and Ella remembered it like it had happened yesterday. It was like a magical moment for her.

They had gone to the square for the Sunset Celebration that took place every night at the pier at the end of Duval Street. Josie and Michael had come along too, but they went out to eat while Seth and Ella found a spot to view the sunset, which looked like it was going to be spectacular. The pier was crowded that night, so Seth stood behind Ella as they watched the sun sink into the sea.

When Ella turned around to leave, Seth stood in place, and before she knew it, his lips gently met hers. Her mind wondered if this was too soon or if she should have let him kiss her at all since he would be leaving to go back home. The moment had happened so fast but had felt so right. The feeling she experienced with his soft touch was not one she could part with, nor did she ever want it to leave. It didn't matter that people were standing all around them. For Ella, at that moment, it was only the two of them standing on the pier.

From that night on, Ella found that all her free time was with Seth, if possible. But the day he left to go back to Montana was so hard. She honestly didn't think it would have affected her like it did. This was just a fling, she had kept telling herself over and over. Yes, they had shared passionate kisses, holding hands as they explored the city. But that was it. Nothing more.

Ella knew that she had much more important things in her life to concentrate on. When he left, she would get back to her studies and finally secure that job she wanted. But as she watched Seth walk away to board the plane, her heart sank. She had fallen for him in such a short time that it was hard for her to grasp her feelings as he disappeared around the corner.

Ella stashed her trash in her lunch tote and headed back to the boat. As she neared the dock, the passengers were boarding, ready for their excursion to view the creatures in the ocean. But then she heard an alert notification on her phone. She looked at the screen, and a smile lit up her face. It was Seth.

As she quickly read the message, the smile on her face grew bigger. Just knowing that he was thinking of her made her excited, but it also gave her an idea, even if it was a bit crazy. And if she could pull it off, she would be one happy girl.

3

As Seth boarded the plane and placed his carry-on in the over-head compartment, his exhilaration was over the top. In just a few hours, he would see Ella. The thought of her honey-touched skin, the long, dark hair that framed her delicate face, and her beautiful smile that could light up a room had him thrilled. The best part was that he was going to surprise her.

Actually, it would be a surprise to his dad and Josie too since he told no one where he was going – except Charlie, whom he swore to secrecy. Charlie even held up his right hand and said it was a promise, laughing the whole time, telling Seth to make sure he didn't come back married. Seth assured him he didn't have to worry about that, but as he sat in the plane, getting ready to head to sunny Florida, he couldn't help but think about Charlie's words. What would it be like to be married to Ella? Just the thought of it made him smile broadly.

Seth sent Ella a text as he got to the airport, but it was one of their normal, everyday messages, always hoping that her day would be nice and how much he missed her. He asked about the warm weather since it was snowing for him and inquired how her school project was going. It took all his willpower not to let her know that later today, he would be able to hold her in his arms. Instead, Seth laid his head back on the seat and imagined how she would react the moment she saw him.

If the plane arrived in Key West on time, he should get there just before her dinner shift at the restaurant. Ella had texted back to him that it was going to be a full day because once she was finished working, her final project for her degree was her main priority. She even went so far as to tell him that she wouldn't be able to talk on the phone, like they planned. Seth hoped seeing him didn't put too much of a wrinkle in her plans. He might be with her in Key West, but he would make sure she had time for school because it was so important to her.

After making his plane reservation, Seth immediately made plans to stay in a nearby hotel, so most of his time could be spent with Ella. When she was working, he would go surprise his dad and Josie in Marathon. It was all arranged, and he couldn't wait to see the crystal-clear water and wear flip-flops instead of the snow boots he had left behind at his house.

Seth had several legs to this journey, flying out of the Great Falls Airport. At least he didn't have many layovers. During the longest part of his trip, he worked non-stop on his laptop, wrapping up a few work projects before he got to the Keys. He didn't want any of his time in the islands taken away because of something he might have pending back at the ranch. Once he was on the final plane heading to Key West, he closed his eyes, determined to take a quick nap, but the excitement of being so close to the Keys kept him awake. Before he knew it, the captain of the plane came over the speaker announcing their descent into Key West.

Seth looked out the window to see the turquoise water below, and his body relaxed, but at the same time, anticipation raced through him. Ella. He didn't think he could get to the rental car counter fast enough. And he couldn't wait to see the look on her face when she saw him standing at the dock.

It didn't take long till Seth was parking the car close to Duvall Street. As he walked toward the boat dock, he wished he had brought flowers or something that he could give to Ella. But then he saw the boat was docked and passengers disembarking. He stood at the edge, waiting for the crew of the boat to step off. Different people came and left, but he didn't see her. Seth waited a bit longer, but when he saw someone he recognized as Ella's co-worker from his previous trip, he had to ask where she was.

"Hi, I'm Ella's friend. Not sure if you remember me," Seth said to the man as he walked off the boat.

"How could I forget! I kept telling Ella we should put you to work 'cause you were here so much," the man laughed.

"Is Ella still on board?"

"No, she's gone."

"Gone? Home?" Seth asked, his voice faltering a bit.

The man started laughing and shook his head. "As far as I know, she is on a plane headed to Montana to see you! So, what are you doing here in Key West?"

As Ella stepped off the plane, even though she was inside the building, she felt a definite chill in the air. Looking out the airport window, the sight of snow made her face light up like a child receiving the very gift they wanted. It was beautiful, and with the contrast of the bright blue sky, she was mesmerized. But she needed to get a car and find her way to Seth's ranch. She couldn't wait to see the look on his face! As Ella continued to stare at the beautiful scene before her, a small bit of panic rose inside her. Suddenly the thought occurred to her that she had never driven in snow, and she certainly didn't know where she was going.

Ella sat down on the closest chair and took out her phone. With a quick look at the map, she saw that Seth's ranch was about an hour away from the Great Falls airport. In all her excitement about her trip, she hadn't thought about her transportation once she arrived in Montana. She wanted to get to Seth but driving in the snow? The anxiety began to swell inside, but she quickly suppressed it. Just the thought of Seth's face when she showed up on his doorstep made her smile. At least, Ella hoped he would be happy to see her.

Instantly, new doubts plagued her, ones that she had not thought of before. What if he had a girlfriend here? What if the messages they had sent back and forth had only meant to forge a strong friendship, not the romance she read into every word Seth had written? What had she done? The exhilaration she had felt only moments ago was turning into apprehension.

Ella's ringing cell phone broke the string of negative thoughts that marched one after another through her mind. One look at the screen showed it was Seth. Should she tell him she was here and let him pick her up or still try to surprise him? Well, her just being in Montana would surprise him enough, she thought. She looked at the snow, knowing she didn't know what to do.

"Hello," Ella said as calmly as she could.

"Hi there! Where are you?" Ella could sense by the way Seth was talking that something was not quite right, but she couldn't figure out what it was.

"Um, where are you?" she asked quickly, still trying to figure out the correct words to say to surprise him.

"I'm standing on Duval Street."

"What!" Ella exclaimed.

"Yeah, I've been waiting for you to come off the boat tour for some time. But then I was informed that you took a vacation. You wouldn't mind telling me where you are, would you?"

Ella still couldn't believe what she had just heard, nor the laughter that came in response to Seth's words.

"Well, I'm looking at some very beautiful snow, something I've never seen in person before. I think I'm in a place called the Great Falls Airport," Ella giggled.

"I can't believe this!" Seth said, laughter in his voice now too.

"Maybe we can say that great minds think alike?" Ella asked. "I wanted to surprise you. You've seen where I live and I thought I would come here to see what was so special about Montana. I haven't been outside yet, but it looks stunning."

"I can't believe you are in Montana," Seth said. "I can get on the next plane and be there probably tomorrow. That is, if you want to see my part of the country. Or you could fly back home."

"Are you kidding? I want you to come back here. I can't wait to go play out in the snow!" Ella said. "Except there is one problem."

"What's that?"

"In my haste to surprise you, I didn't plan all the elements of my trip thoroughly. I've never been in snow, much less driven in it. Plus, I never checked how far you were from the airport. I remembered you telling me that you flew out of Great Falls, so that is where I came. I see now that your ranch is about an hour away. Should I just stay in a hotel close by here till you get back?" Ella asked.

"No way. I'll make a call and have Charlie come and get you. He can take you to my house. Just make yourself at home till I get back. I'll try to leave today, except I have to say, it feels mighty good down here. When I left the ranch, there was about eight inches of snow on the ground."

"This is only eight inches! It looks like feet to me," Ella exclaimed.

"Then I have a lot to teach my island girl when I get there," Seth said. "Stay put, and I'll call you after I get in touch with Charlie. Plus, I'll let you know when I should be back. I can't believe we did this."

"I can't either," Ella said, still laughing. "I wonder if it means something?"

"Like what?" Seth asked.

"I don't know. Let's say we talk about it when you get back."

Ella clicked the disconnect button and smiled. He had been thinking of her as much as she was him. He even said the words "my island girl". To her, this was like a sign from above. Maybe Seth was the man that was meant to be in her life. Her mom had always told her that she would know when the right one came along, and with Seth, it was so easy. Only now, she had to wait a little bit longer to see him. But she knew it would be worth the wait.

4

"Hey, boss," Charlie said. "Calling so soon? I told you I could handle everything here. You worry too much, like your dad."

"I know you can take care of the ranch with your eyes closed. No, I'm actually calling you for a favor. Ella is in Montana!"

"Who?"

Seth sighed. "Ella, the woman I came to see in Florida."

"The girl off the boat? From Key West? What do you mean she is here? At the ranch?" Charlie asked, one question after another.

"No, she is at the Great Falls Airport. It seems that we had the same thing in mind. She was trying to surprise me with a trip to the ranch, and I flew here to surprise her." Suddenly, Seth heard Charlie's loud laugh pealing through the phone's speaker.

"Man, you two must have it real bad. I thought this was just some casual thing with you, but this girl must be mighty special. Seth's finally got a girl!" Charlie exclaimed loudly into the phone.

"You sound like I'm a hermit or something," Seth said with exasperation at being teased. "Right now, I need your help. Ella is at the airport. She's never been up north or in that type of weather. She was going to rent a car and drive to the ranch but is scared to on account of the snow. I need you to pick her up and take her to my place at the ranch. She can stay there till I get back tomorrow."

"No problem, boss. But how will I know what she looks like?"

"Going to send you a picture." Seth quickly found a photo he had taken of Ella when they went to the Bahia Honda Beach and sent it.

"I remember this pic. You showed it to me when you got back from the Keys. I don't think I'll be able to miss this beauty."

"Just remember you're married, Charlie," Seth said.

"Hey, just stating facts. I'm happy at home, you know that."

"I do. Guess I'm just a bit protective."

"Honestly, I don't blame you. But out of all the guys she has to pick from in the Keys, she comes to see you? Might need to get her head checked."

"Ha, ha," Seth sighed. "Listen, let me give her a call and tell her what's going on. Then I've got to find a flight home. I'm heading to the airport as soon as I can get packed, which shouldn't take very long. I'll update you when I can."

"Don't worry about Ella. We'll make sure she is fine and show her around a bit while she waits for you, lover boy."

Seth rolled his eyes but smiled at Charlie's statement. "Thanks. I owe you Charlie." As soon as Seth hit the disconnect button, he called Ella to let her know all the details. Now, if only he could snap his fingers and be back at the ranch. And be with Ella.

As he packed, changing clothes from the shorts and flip-flops he had on to his jeans and cowboy boots, he suddenly had a picture of Ella in the snow. He imagined her bundled up in a thick coat, scarf around her neck, and her beautiful black-brown tresses flowing out from a chunky crocheted hat. Jeans that fit her snuggly with her own set of boots. The picture was very different from what he had ever seen her in before, and the thought of her was sexier than ever.

Seth still remembered the first time they went to the beach, and he saw her in a bikini. It took all his willpower to keep his wits about him because he felt like he was sitting beside a cover model, with the fire engine-red bathing suit accentuating her caramel-colored skin. But to see her in his part of the country, in the snow? His willpower was sure to be tested yet again.

The Key West Airport was crowded with late afternoon vacationers heading back home. As Seth looked around, he wondered if he would be able to get a flight. There were so many people surrounding him.

"I don't have any available seats till tomorrow afternoon. Then that is only to Atlanta. Everything is booked to Great Falls till the following morning."

Seth looked at the agent and shut his eyes. This was what he feared. "Nothing at all? What about standby for tonight?"

"I can put you on standby, but you'll probably end up staying here pretty late, then have to find a hotel for the evening. Only other option would be to drive to Miami for a late flight to Atlanta this evening. Then I can get you on the morning flight to Great Falls," the woman said from behind the counter.

"I'll take it!" Seth said with no hesitation.

The airline employee printed out the necessary papers and handed them to Seth. "If you plan on making that flight, you need to hustle. It's a three-hour drive to Miami, and this flight leaves in four."

"Thanks!" Seth turned quickly, grabbed his rolling suitcase, and sprinted toward the car rental counter. Within thirty minutes, he was on Hwy 1, driving just above the speed limit.

He loved driving through the Keys, with all the spectacular scenery everywhere he looked, but right now, he was focused on making that flight to Atlanta. He had to get to Montana and to Ella.

✲ ✲ ✲

Ella sat in the airport, her luggage by her side. She had already taken out the coat from her tote bag to prepare for the outside winter wonderland. After she got the call from Seth, she couldn't help but laugh at the situation. How had she and Seth been thinking about the exact same thing? They had probably crossed paths somewhere in the sky. But what made her heart swell was something that her mother was sure to say if she knew what was going on.

"It's a sign, Ella."

"What do you mean, Momma?"

"This boy loves you. He is yours."

Ella could almost hear the conversation, it came to her so clearly in her mind. And if her mother's words were true, Ella had a lot to think about. Her attraction to Seth was just that at first – a fascination with this adorable man. But when he left to come here, back to Montana, Ella knew there was more to this relationship than just a casual tourist she would never see again.

Now, Ella was in his world. After she heard Seth would be here tomorrow, she had peered out every window she could find to see more of the world around her. She thought about stepping through the airport doors and walking around but decided to wait till someone named "Charlie" was there to pick her up. Not that she was nervous, but she had never experienced weather like this and wasn't sure what to expect. Her friends had teased her about getting frostbite or getting lost in the woods, never to be seen again. Ella had taken it all in stride, knowing that Seth wouldn't let anything happen to her.

But as Ella continued to gaze at the view through the windows, she knew she was very much out of her comfort zone. For the second time since she began this journey, her nerves were jittery as she thought about all the "what ifs" that could happen.

"Pardon me, ma'am, but are you Ella Cummings?"

Ella stepped out of the scenarios that kept playing in her mind to see a tall man dressed in jeans and a flannel shirt, with a thick coat on top. She saw wisps of grey hair coming from underneath a cowboy hat, and the boots he wore looked comfortable but worn. He had a sweet smile that reminded her of her father.

"I am. Are you Charlie?" Ella asked, smiling at the man.

"That I am. It seems you and Seth got your wires crossed just a bit." Charlie chuckled a little, and Ella had to laugh with him.

"That appears to be the case. I guess you could say we both were surprised."

"Oh, you could say that, for sure," Charlie continued. "I hear that you've never been up here before. Never even been in the snow or mountains. That so?"

"Yes, sir."

"Hey, stop that 'sir' nonsense. The name is Charlie. 'Sir' sounds too old, and I'm a young'un."

Ella could not help but smile at this gentle man standing before her.

"Well, Charlie, you're right," Ella said. Then she looked sideways to the window again. "It's so beautiful."

"If you think that parking lot is pretty, then you are in for a special treat when we get to the ranch. If snow is what you wanted to see, then we definitely have that for you, and we're expecting more this evening. Wouldn't be surprised if we had a blizzard warning."

Ella cheerful demeanor vanished at his words.

"Blizzard? Aren't those dangerous?"

"Only if you happen to be dumb enough to get yourself caught outside in one, but that don't happen around here. Besides, you'll be staying at Seth's house at the ranch, and it's mighty nice and warm. Don't you worry yourself. Once the snow is settled, it's really pretty up here. Especially with the mountains close by."

"Mountains," Ella said softly. She had seen snow-covered mountains only in magazines or the internet. To experience them up close would be exciting. But it would be even better to experience everything with Seth.

"Put your coat on now because it's a bit cold. Only going to get to thirty degrees today, which is actually warm this time of year," Charlie said as he repositioned his hat on his head.

"Thirty for a high?" Ella asked incredulously.

"What was the temperature when you left the Keys?"

"Warm enough that I was able to wear flip-flops and shorts." Ella smiled.

"Well, Ella, welcome to Montana," Charlie said, taking her suitcase from her, and they both headed out of the airport terminal doors.

5

Seth walked as fast as he could, dodging people that stood in his way. He had only a few minutes to reach the terminal gate, or he would miss that all important flight to Atlanta.

His drive through the Keys had been beautiful but rushed. He pushed past the speed limit, watching every corner for the highway patrol, and barely made it to the airport on time. As he passed by his dad's house in Marathon, Seth wished he could have stopped to say "hello", but he didn't have time. Instead, he called to tell his dad and Josie his part of the strange but funny situation between him and Ella. Seth could only listen as his dad and stepmom laughed and told him to get his butt to Miami. Seth said he would make it in time and promised to be back for a visit real soon.

"Hi there," the flight attendant said as Seth walked on board. "You seem to be the last one to arrive. Looks like you have a seat in first class."

And he did. It was the only seat available to Atlanta, and Seth wasn't about to wait for another plane. But as he took his seat, the extra money was worth it. With all the rushing from packing, driving, and running through the airport, he needed some time to just relax.

Seth had wanted to call Ella once more before boarding the plane, but there had been no time. At least he had talked to her for a bit while he drove through the little Florida islands. He couldn't wait to get back to Montana, to show her his place, like she had done while he was in the Keys. He only hoped that she had warm clothing because it was cold with more snow expected, something she wasn't used to.

Seth settled in and laid his head back in the seat. As the plane lifted off the ground, he saw the beautiful aqua water and sun-drenched beaches. Part of him wanted to dig his toes into the sand and swim in the ocean. But right now, all he saw in his mind was a beautiful, dark-haired girl bundled up with a coat and scarf, waiting for him in Montana.

Ella couldn't believe the winter wonderland she saw out the truck windows. It was breathtaking no matter which way she looked. Everything was white and covered in a blanket of snow.

Off in the distance, she saw huge, majestic mountains topped with snow that seemed to flow down the sides. It looked like a picture or postcard.

As they drove toward the ranch, she was more than happy that Charlie had come to pick her up. Even if Seth had been here, Ella would have to had called him from the airport to pick her up instead of surprising him on his doorstep. The roads were slick and icy, but Charlie drove them like this was just a normal day. And for him, Ella guessed, it was. He was used to this weather, but not her.

"Whatcha think so far?" Charlie asked as they continued down the road.

"It's beautiful! I've only seen something like this in books or online. But it's so cold," Ella said, wrapping her arms around herself. The coat was helping, but she knew now that she wasn't prepared for the weather here. She would definitely have to get some clothing, maybe even boots because the sneakers and socks that she thought would be sufficient were not keeping her toes warm. Thanks goodness, the truck had a great heater.

Charlie laughed. "Honestly, this is normal. Like I said, a high of thirty degrees is nice this time of year. How long are you going to be here?"

"A week."

"Then you'll get to see some real Montana winter weather. That storm coming through here tonight is supposed to bring our temperatures down quite a bit. I think the high tomorrow is around fourteen."

"Fourteen degrees?" Ella exclaimed.

"Don't worry. You're going to be just fine."

"Think I might have to do a bit of shopping. I thought the clothing I brought would be fine, but I'm shivering right now, even with the heater on."

"I can turn it up a bit higher. You just aren't used to this, that's all. But I'm sure Seth will take you into town and get you some stuff. Probably need a warmer coat, hat, and scarf, for sure, with some good boots."

"That will give me some souvenirs to take home." Ella grinned.

"Maybe you'll be able to use them again."

"I hope so," Ella said shyly, turning to look out the side window again.

"Well, here we are," Charlie said as they turned onto a side road, and Ella saw the sign: Garner Ranch. But what caught Ella's attention was the field to the side. It looked like thousands of cows in the field, with a large building in the distance. How the animals were not frozen in place, she had no idea, but from a distance, it seemed like they were eating something. There were even little ones among the large animals! This amazed her because she didn't know how anything could exist in the outside weather.

As they continued down the road, she saw a large, fenced-in area with many horses – so many, she couldn't count.

"Seth said this was a cattle ranch. That means cows, right? What about the horses?"

"We have steers and cows, but the horses are what the cowboys use."

"There are still cowboys?" Ella asked. "I thought that just a myth."

Charlie couldn't help but laugh. "Yep, we have plenty of them to herd the cattle when its time. Don't mean any disrespect, but you really are an island girl, huh?"

Ella smiled, embarrassed. "I guess so. My world is sun, beaches, and boats on crystal-clear waters. I ride a bicycle practically everywhere, and I never need a coat. I think I only wear a sweater or jacket a few times a year. Maybe use one occasionally, if I'm in a restaurant and it's a bit chilly."

"Well, I hope you like it up here, and I know Seth feels the same way. I don't think he has stopped talking about you or Florida since he got home from seeing his father. I had planned on getting an earful about Michael and Josie, and instead, I heard about everything you two did."

Ella blushed. So, Seth had thought about her, just like she had about him.

"Seth would probably be a bit upset if he knew I told you that, so let's keep this conversation between the two of us, okay?" Charlie asked.

"No problem," Ella laughed.

"Well, we are here. This is Seth's house, or should I say Michael's. But anyway, we're here."

Ella looked at the grand house before her. It looked like one of those homes on a Christmas card. It was a beautiful two-story home made of wood, logs, and stone. Even though it was covered in snow, the walkways and driveway had been neatly cleared, showing the inviting front porch, with its rocking chairs. There was a large detached garage next to the house, with a covered walkway. And the best part was the view of the stunning mountains behind the house. They were still far away, but they were so large that Ella felt she could possibly walk to their base.

But what surprised her the most was how big the house was. Did Seth live here by himself? A house like this in the Keys was more than a mansion! This was the kind of house that someone built if they bought a private island.

"It's so large! Does Seth live here by himself?" Ella asked curiously.

"Sure does, unless someone needs a place to stay. Like, if we are working late or the weather gets too bad. But that's rare. Come on, let's get you inside, and I'll show you around. Plus, we need to make sure Seth has something for you to eat. That boy isn't too good about keeping food in the cabinets, like his Dad did."

6

Ella knew she must have looked like a deer caught in headlights when she walked into the house. The deep cold she felt only moments ago in the short walk from the truck to the house was now gone. The warm house was beyond stunning.

Beautiful wood in varying shades, from light to dark, graced the house from the ceiling above, with its exposed wooden beams, to the floor, with its wooden planks. The walls looked like one log stacked on top of another, so seamless that Ella was mesmerized. In the family room, there was a floor-to-ceiling fireplace, with windows of the same size on each side that allowed her to see the mountains outside. A fire was already glowing from the opening among the stones, making the area seem even cozier than she could have ever imagined. The entire house was open, as she was able to look from room to room.

"Let me take your stuff upstairs. Seth said to make sure you got the room next to his because it has a great view of the ranch," Charlie said.

"I can't believe this house. It's beautiful!"

"Seth's dad, Michael, designed it. He loves this home, and when he told me he was moving to the Keys, I couldn't believe it. But I guess that's what falling in love does to you."

Ella and Charlie turned as they heard a knock on the door, and a tall, handsome man entered the house. At first glance, Ella saw a resemblance between the newcomer and Charlie, but she wasn't completely sure.

"Hey, Dad. I thought that was your truck. Having a bit of trouble in the West pasture, and I..." The man stopped short at the sight of Ella.

"Ella, this is my son, Tanner. Tanner, this is Ella, Seth's friend from Key West. She's going to be staying here for a while, waiting for Seth to get back."

Tanner came over and stood before Ella. His gaze unnerved her a bit, making her feel like she was on display. But Tanner was quite good-looking. He looked almost like a male model, with chestnut hair and a chiseled jawline. He was taller than his father but very muscular. As Tanner came closer, Ella definitely saw the resemblance between father and son. It was in their eyes and the way they smiled.

"Well, hi there." Tanner extended his hand, which Ella took to shake, but Tanner abruptly turned to his dad. "Wait a minute. Seth said he was going to Florida."

Charlie started laughing. "He was there for probably all of about three hours. Now, he is on his way back because who he went to see came to see him instead."

Tanner laughed and looked at Ella once more. "Seriously? You came to surprise Seth?"

"Yes, but it seems we both had the same thing in mind."

"This your first time to Montana?"

"Yep. I've never been anywhere past Atlanta, Georgia," Ella said shyly, almost embarrassed that she wasn't much of a traveler.

"So, how do you like our snow? I'm sure this is quite different than those islands Seth talks about all the time."

"It's very cold, which I'm certainly not used to, but it's gorgeous. Like I told your dad, this is something I've seen in pictures. Everywhere I look seems like a postcard to me. Even this house!"

"So, when is Seth getting back?" Tanner asked, clearly directing the question to his father but not taking his eyes off Ella.

"Should be here tomorrow."

"Then we need to make sure you are taken care of till he gets back," Tanner said, now giving his full attention to Ella. "Does Seth have any food in the house? He is famous for having nothing but junk, if anything at all." Before Ella knew it, Tanner was in the kitchen opening cabinets and looking into the refrigerator.

"Seth and Tanner have been friends since they were little. But when Seth finally moved back here, it seems wherever you see one, you see the other," Charlie said. "Listen, I'll be right back."

Ella watched as Charlie took her luggage upstairs and then looked over to see Tanner continuing to check out the kitchen cabinets.

"Like I thought. Nothing. Need to go to the grocery store and pick up a few things for you. Then I'll make you some dinner tonight. I know you just got here, but you want to ride to the store? That way, you can get some food you want instead of us trying to decide for you," Tanner asked with a smile.

"Oh, I'm sure I can find something here," Ella said, coming into the kitchen.

"I don't think so." Tanner stood back and opened a few cabinets, then the refrigerator. Ella couldn't help but laugh.

"I guess you and your dad were right. Does Seth ever eat?"

"Yes, but we usually bug my mom. She loves to cook, but she is out of town for a few nights. So, what about that ride to the grocery store?"

"I guess I'll put my coat back on and brave the cold," Ella said.

"Ella and I are going to ride to the grocery store and get some food," Tanner said as his father came around the corner.

"No food?"

"Nope."

"Thought so. I came by and lit the fireplace before I headed to the airport. Forgot that boy doesn't go to the store often. Too bad your mother is away."

"That's what I was just telling Ella." Tanner continued to grin at her.

"You two be careful. Weather is okay right now, but that storm is coming through soon."

"We'll be back in a few," Tanner said and motioned for Ella to follow him.

Before she knew it, Ella was leaving the warmth of the house and heading back out into the cold winter weather. Though the air stung her exposed skin, she still couldn't get enough of the surroundings. But this time, she noticed that their sunny skies were now covered in clouds.

This was a whole different world for her, and she couldn't wait for Seth to get back, to show it all to her.

7

Seth tried for the fifth time to call Ella but received only her voicemail. He hoped she was okay and finally decided to call Charlie, hoping to reach him to at least give him the news.

"Hi, kid. You 'bout home?" Charlie said as he answered his phone.

"Been trying to call Ella. Is everything okay?" Seth asked anxiously.

"Sure. Got her settled in at the house and then she went to the grocery store with Tanner. Son, you've got to keep food in those cabinets. If we had one of those bad blizzards, you'd starve."

"Tanner took her to the grocery store?" Seth asked, a shockwave running through him at the words.

"Yep. Told them to be careful with the snow we got coming."

Trying to remember the reason for his call after hearing Charlie's words, Seth finally calmed his racing mind. "Well, that's why I've been trying to call Ella. My flight was canceled for tomorrow morning because of the weather. There is a possibility that I might get out of here tomorrow afternoon, but they said I might only get to Seattle. It depends on how much snow we get up there. I can't believe three days of her trip will already be gone by the time I get to the ranch," Seth said longingly.

"We'll take care of her. She's a sweet girl. We'll show her around a bit but leave the nice stuff for you two. That way, she won't get bored. But if this snow is anything they say it's going to be, we'll probably be inside, watching TV, which sounds mighty good to me right now."

"How's the ranch?" Seth asked, though he was more concerned about Ella. And the fact that she was with his womanizing best friend.

"Everything is fine, boss, so don't sweat it. Just get back here to be with your gal," Charlie said. "I'll tell her you called, but keep trying her cell phone. I'm sure you'll get her soon."

"Thanks, Charlie," Seth said and clicked the disconnect button.

Of all the people he knew, Ella was with his best friend. And that should be okay, Seth thought. But Seth had seen over the years how Tanner was with the women in his life, and there had been many. All Seth knew was that Tanner had better not try to work his ways on Ella.

Where was this jealousy coming from? He trusted Ella, and his best friend wouldn't do anything to hurt him right? Seth only remembered how women seemed to be drawn to Tanner like a moth to a flame. Seth had always laughed about it in the past, but now, things were different. Tanner was with someone that was so special to Seth that he didn't realize the depth of his feelings for this woman till this crazy mix-up. He had never felt this spark of jealousy before in his life.

Hadn't Ella just made a huge trip just to surprise him? At that thought, Seth smiled. And she had been a bit aloof the first few times they were together, so there was no way she would succumb to Tanner's charming ways. Ella was very independent, but how they had been having the same thoughts, Seth didn't know. To him, that was a sure sign that they did, indeed, have something more than a close friendship.

Seth tried once more to call Ella, and this time, he wasn't disappointed.

"Seth?"

"Hi there! Been trying to call you," he said, loving just hearing the sound of her voice.

"Sorry I missed your calls, but I was doing a bit of grocery shopping," Ella said, a smile in her voice. "Do you ever eat at home?"

"I know. Not much there. But I'm usually at Charlie's house because Mary cooks some great meals."

"Mary?"

"Charlie's wife. I'm either there or at the diner close by. If I don't feel like going out, I'll just snack on whatever is available. But I do know how to cook," Seth said, feeling so much reassurance just hearing her voice.

"Well, that's good because I'm picking up a few staples for your kitchen. That way, when you get here, we can have some homemade meals. Maybe even do some cooking together. Your kitchen is wonderful! I've never seen one so nice and big! I can't wait till you get here. What time will you be here tomorrow?"

"That's why I was calling. I'm in Atlanta, and my flight for tomorrow morning got cancelled. I can get to Seattle, but then I'm stuck until this new storm blows through."

"Oh, no!"

Seth heard the disappointment in Ella's voice. "I promise, when I do get home, we're going to have a great time. There is so much I want to show you, even if there is a bunch of snow. Ever been on a snowmobile?"

Ella laughed. "Seth, remember I haven't been up north, period. Seeing this snowy weather is just amazing. You have to remember that my winters are an occasional sweater and maybe a pair of jeans. Oh, and maybe some sneakers. Speaking of which,

I do need to shop for some clothing. Tanner is going to take me by a little store on the way home so I can get a few things, mainly some boots. My shoes aren't doing the trick of keeping my feet warm."

There was his name again. Tanner. Seth never knew he could feel this kind of irritation about his best friend, but with Ella involved, he did. Just knowing that he was shopping with her, taking her around his place and his town had Seth on edge. Maybe he could rent a car once he arrived in Seattle tomorrow, but that probably wasn't the brightest idea either. It would be a very long trip with the winter weather. He would have to wait and see.

"Just get what you need – groceries, clothing, anything. I'll pay for all of it when I get back."

"No, I got it."

"Really, I want to. I just wish I was already there. To see you."

"I can't wait for you to get here. I'm ready to see your world, Seth."

"And I can't wait to show you."

Ella put her cell phone back in her coat pocket and looked at the contents of her grocery cart before her. She had all the necessary items that she could think of to stock the cabinets and refrigerator till Seth arrived. There were some simple things she knew she could cook, mostly in the microwave she had seen sitting on Seth's kitchen counter.

"You sure you have everything?" Tanner asked, coming to stand close beside her.

"Think so. Even threw in some snacks too."

"Well, I have the makings for s'mores."

"I've always heard of those but never tried them."

"Are you kidding? Then maybe we will remedy that later on," Tanner said, placing the items in Ella's cart. "And I'll pay for this."

"No, I've got it," Ella said.

"No, let me. Let's just say it's a 'Welcome to Montana' gift."

Before Ella knew it, Tanner gave her a quick wink and swiftly took control of the grocery cart. He was definitely charming, but all she could think about was Seth. She said a silent prayer that he would be here as soon as possible.

8

The stop at the clothing store was just what Ella needed next. The boots she purchased were so warm, she was sure she would never take them off. She also found a beautiful, thick scarf with a matching hat and then a set of gloves guaranteed to keep her fingers nice and toasty.

As she had made her way around the store, she spied a few sweaters and another pair of denim jeans, to round out the wardrobe she had brought with her. She had no idea if or when she would wear them again, but for the time being, she had no choice if she wanted to stay warm.

The ride back to the ranch was nice, with Tanner giving her a small tour of the town and some nearby landmarks. He even shared stories with Ella of him and Seth while they were learning the ways of the ranch. Seth had told Ella how he had moved here to live with his father as soon as he had graduated from high school, but Tanner had grown up on the ranch. He was a true cowboy in every sense of the word.

"Those clouds are looking kind of ominous. Glad we're back," Tanner said. He opened the truck door and took most of the grocery bags in his hands.

Ella looked up at the sky above to see dark gray clouds. For some reason, it reminded her of the tropical storms they experienced in the Keys occasionally, but these clouds looked a bit thicker. Then a huge snowflake floated before her face.

"It's snowing!" Ella stood entranced by the sight. The bags in her hands slid to the ground, and she held her hand out, just as one of the white ice crystals landed in the center of it. It was beautiful and delicate, melting almost immediately as it touched her skin.

"Let's get your stuff inside before this snow starts coming down heavier," Tanner called from the porch.

His voice brought Ella back to the present. She looked around and saw the snow was beginning to fall faster, and she just smiled. Then she quickly grabbed her camera out of her coat pocket and began to snap some pictures. She had to send these to her parents because they would never believe that she was standing in snow, much less watching it fall all around her. But she quickly remembered that she hadn't told them about her trip, much less about Seth.

They were always encouraging her to date, but Ella told her mother and father that she had other goals to keep her busy. Ella knew, though, that her parents would adore Seth. She just wasn't ready to let them know about him till she was sure about her feelings and his toward her. This trip would surely let her know.

"Here, I got them." Tanner said. He was suddenly by Ella's side, scooping up the bags on the ground all around her.

"I'm sorry," Ella said quickly. "It's just so pretty. I've never seen snow fall."

"Then you are in for a treat, especially later on. It's nice right now, but soon, it will be so thick, you won't be able to see a foot in front of you. At least, that's the forecast for tonight."

"Your dad mentioned something earlier about a bad storm this evening."

"We have a blizzard warning, but they say it should only last overnight. Hoping this will blow through fast."

"Sounds like some of the bad storms we've had in the islands. But I have to say, this is much prettier than heavy rain." Ella continued to watch the flakes fall, smiling. "Is this the storm that's keeping Seth from getting a flight?"

"Yep. Come on, let get inside. Maybe later, I'll challenge you to a snowball fight, if it's not too bad," Tanner said, Ella on his heels.

"Maybe." Ella had thought about the things she wanted to do when she got to Montana, but she wanted to share them with Seth, not Tanner. Tanner was nice and had been the perfect gentleman, but Seth was the one she had come all this way to spend time with. And Ella couldn't wait till she got the call that he would be here soon.

✼ ✼ ✼

"At this time, that is far as I can guarantee a flight," the counter agent told Seth. He'd been hoping that she would give him better news.

"Well, I'll take it. At least it's a little bit closer to home," Seth said as nicely as he could, though he was frustrated inside. But once he arrived in Seattle, maybe the flights would be open again. As much as he wanted to hurry home and be with Ella, he knew flying in this weather wasn't safe. But that didn't help when the person he wanted to see most was sitting in his house, probably with his best friend.

I trust Tanner, right? Seth asked himself once again. Of course, he did. Tanner would not hurt him. They had been friends for so long. They were like brothers. But there was something that just kept nagging at him. Ella was beautiful, sweet, and kind. She was certainly different than the other girls in his hometown. Seth knew for someone like Tanner, that would be enticing.

As Seth walked to the gate where he would catch the early-morning plane, he could only hope that Tanner would not make a play for Ella and that he could get home as quickly as possible.

"Hello there." Just hearing Ella's voice was so soothing to him.

"Hi. Just wanted to call you and see how you are."

"You'll be here soon, right?"

"Well, I've got a plane to Seattle in the morning. Once I'm there, I'll see what's available. So many flights are cancelled due to the snowstorm, but it should pass by fast. How is everything there?" Seth asked cautiously.

"Wonderful! It's snowing! I mean, lots and lots! I've never seen anything so pretty," Ella exclaimed.

"That's what I was afraid of," Seth said, a bit crestfallen.

"This is the storm that is keeping you away."

"Yes, but keeping my fingers crossed that I'll have better news tomorrow. There is so much I want to show you when I get home. It's still hard for me to wrap my head around the idea that you are there, in Montana."

"Well, this is something that we'll always remember."

"That's for sure," Seth said, laughing. "Is Tanner still there?"

"Yes. He has been such a big help this afternoon, but I think he is leaving shortly. He helped me get the groceries inside and my other shopping bags. I got so distracted by all the snow falling. I couldn't help but start taking pictures. He mentioned something about a snowball fight, but I doubt it. My toes and fingers are just starting to get warm. Plus, I don't even know how to make a snowball," Ella laughed.

I'm sure Tanner will show you, Seth thought to himself. "We'll definitely have one when I get there. And make a snowman and ride the snowmobile. Maybe even go horseback riding, depending on the conditions. Charlie was going to take care of the ranch since I was supposed to be gone anyway, so when I get home, I'm going to treat it like I'm on vacation while you are there. I just wish I wasn't missing so much time being with you."

"You'll be here soon. Just have this feeling," Ella said softly. "And I really can't wait to see you. It's been a while, but I still remember that man I met on the boat that day. All the time we spent exploring the islands. I have to say that is some of the most fun I've had since I moved to Key West."

With each word she spoke, Seth's desire to get home grew stronger.

"I felt the same way. I really enjoy being with you, Ella. Even the texting and phone calls these last few months have been something I've looked forward to every day." Seth paused, wishing so much that he was already on that plane. "I've got to go. Have to find a comfortable place to sleep in the airport."

"Why don't you get a hotel room?" Ella asked.

"Because I don't want to take a chance on missing that plane in the morning. I'm so ready to be with you, in Montana."

"I'll be waiting."

9

Ella hit the disconnect button and looked out the window. The scene before her was gorgeous, but she felt disappointment welling up inside of her. Seth wasn't here, and if this storm kept up, he wouldn't be here as soon as she had hoped.

During the plane ride to Montana, Ella had imagined all kinds of romantic scenarios when she arrived, one of them being the look on Seth's face when he saw her standing before him. She imagined a passionate kiss, like something out of one of those nostalgic movies. From that point, she had no idea what they would do, but it didn't matter because she would have been with Seth.

"Are you okay?" Tanner came to stand beside her, looking at the snow. It was falling so fast that it looked like a white blanket cascading from the sky. They could no longer see the mountains in the distance or anything in the yard surrounding the house.

"That was Seth. He is sleeping at the airport till he can catch a plane in the morning to Seattle, but after that, he doesn't know when he will get here. I wonder if I should try to meet him in Seattle instead?" Ella thought suddenly.

"Don't think you are going anywhere. That snow out there is like a white-out condition."

"White-out?"

"It's when we can't see any landmarks. Makes it very easy to get lost, and that is something you don't want in a storm like this. You could freeze to death."

Ella looked at Tanner with fear in her eyes. What happened if they were stuck in the house? What if they lost power, like they sometimes do during bad storms in the Keys? Would they freeze?

"Could I get stuck here in the house? What about losing electricity?"

"It could happen, but Seth has a back-up generator, so you will be fine," Tanner said just as the phone in his pocket began to ring.

"I'm going to go unpack," Ella said and made her way up the steps and down the small hallway. She peeked in rooms and loved each one. They were decorated in a masculine, western manner, but it fit with the décor of the rest of the house. It was all so different from the colorful island homes she was used to.

Ella saw an opened door and looked to see her suitcase and tote on the floor next to the bed. So, this was to be her room. As she sat on the big bed, she smiled. It was so cozy all around her.

She sank down into the giant bed that was covered with thick, soft blankets. The room even had its own fireplace, already glowing with a small fire, warming the room.

Charlie must have lit it when he brought my things to the room, Ella thought as she smiled, looking around. It was so romantic, and this made her think of Seth even more.

"Hey there," Tanner said, causing Ella to jump slightly. "Didn't mean to startle you."

"That's okay. I was just looking at everything. It's all so beautiful. So different from where I live, but I love it."

"And if it wasn't snowing so heavily, you'd have another great view of the mountains from this room. But it seems like I have a slight problem," Tanner said.

"What's wrong?"

"Think I might have to sleep on your couch tonight, if that's okay with you. Dad just called, and the roads are too bad to drive. But it seems that the snowfall should last just overnight. They are calling for clear skies tomorrow, but the temperatures are going to be pretty frigid. That means this snow is going to stick around for a while. You came just in time to experience a classic Montana winter storm."

Ella sat on the bed, just staring out the window at the blanket of white.

"Is it okay?" Tanner asked.

"What?"

"I kind of need to stay here."

"Oh, of course. I'm sorry. Just thinking."

"No problem. But let's make some dinner. You bought enough food for an army, or at least it looks that way. I don't think I've ever seen so much food in Seth's kitchen," Tanner said with a laugh. "Maybe we could fix some kind of island dish."

"Well, I know some, but I really want something else. It's a recipe from my mom that isn't from the islands at all. How about some beef stroganoff?" Ella asked.

"Wow, that sounds good. So, you like to cook?"

Ella laughed. If Tanner could see the size of her kitchen, he would know her cooking was sparse.

"I like to cook, but that doesn't mean I do it too often. Working two jobs keeps me on the go. Plus, finishing school."

"Man, Seth never said you were that busy."

"I take a break every now and then. Like taking this trip."

"Well, get comfortable. I'll make sure to bring in some firewood before it gets any worse outside, then we will tackle dinner together."

"Sounds good," Ella said.

Tanner stacked the logs next to the fireplace and even brought in extra ones for the fireplace in Ella's room. His head was swimming with all kinds of thoughts, and they all seemed to be about Ella. Not that he would ever hurt his friend, but Ella captured his attention every second they were together. The feelings he was having were so different than he had experienced with other women. He could see why Ella was all Seth could practically talk about. Tanner couldn't help but admit that he was glad he got stuck here. The thought of having dinner with Ella was exciting. She was beautiful, sweet, and her bubbly personality made her so enticing.

Ella entered the room, with her dark hair pulled up into a high ponytail, exposing soft, tanned skin. She had on a pair of sweatpants and a sweater that hugged her curves so well that Tanner couldn't help what he was thinking. At that moment, he knew that as enjoyable as this evening would be, it was going to be difficult too. To be so near this girl he was obviously attracted to and not give in to the desire to see just where the evening could lead to would be difficult.

"Now, that's a lot of firewood," Ella said as she peered over at the stack of wood near the fireplace.

"With the way that snow is coming down, I didn't want to have to go back out there tonight."

"We do have a heater, right?" Ella asked cautiously.

Tanner laughed. "Yeah, it's on right now. Believe me, you would know if it wasn't working. But the fireplaces help too by cutting down on the how hard the furnace has to run. There's enough wood for your room too."

"'Thanks!"

"Ready to do some cooking? I hope so because I'm starving!" Tanner said quickly to help squash the tension he was feeling being in the room with Ella.

"Definitely!"

Tanner watched as Ella went through the refrigerator and the bags that were still on the counter, taking out the ingredients she needed to make the recipe she talked about earlier. Tanner took a seat at the kitchen counter and watched her. Every move she made had him thinking more about wanting to get to know her even better. But then he saw a picture of Seth in his mind and shook his head.

"What's wrong?" Ella asked.

Tanner looked at her, embarrassed that he had been caught staring at her. "Nothing. Just hoping this snow isn't any worse than they predicted."

"Sorry you are stuck here with me," Ella said.

Tanner wasn't. He hated to admit it, but he was definitely very attracted to his best friend's girl. He knew what he should do, but with every move Ella made and every word she spoke, it was getting insanely difficult for Tanner to not go around the corner and just envelop her in his arms. He had known Ella all of about five hours, and she had him hooked.

10

Though the bench wasn't comfortable in the least, Seth took his "pillow" made from his coat and stretched out as much as he could to get some sleep. He made sure that his travel bag was securely attached to his wrist in case someone decided they wanted to steal it from him. They wouldn't be able to without waking him, and all the compartments were locked up tight. But Seth knew he probably wouldn't sleep so soundly anyway because he wasn't the only one stuck in the airport for the night. There were plenty of people around him, and they had all found places to curl up and sleep, hoping for planes that would fly tomorrow.

As he closed his eyes, Seth couldn't help but think of Ella, in his house by herself. He hoped that he had cleaned up the place and was glad that she had food to eat now, even if Tanner had been the one to take her. Plus, he knew that Charlie would check on her first thing in the morning, since Ella wasn't used to winter storms.

If only he was there with her. These storms were cozy, even if the weather outside was brutal. As long as you had your provisions, usually including a good book and a fireplace, it was nice. But the thought of spending a storm like this with Ella by his side was completely different. How many times had he been through this scenario in his head already? All he knew was that the more he thought about it, the desire to get home grew stronger and stronger.

* * *

"Wow, you can cook," Tanner said as he took the last bite of beef stroganoff on his plate.

"I can't believe it actually turned out okay. I didn't have my recipe here with me," Ella said, sitting back in the chair. She looked once again out the window, but now, instead of seeing falling snow, the window was pitch-black.

"Did you doubt your skills?"

"No, I remembered the recipe, but it's been a long time since I cooked it. Like I said, I don't have much time at home to cook, but when I do, I love it. My mother loves to cook, so I guess it runs in the family."

"So, your parents live in Key West too?" Tanner asked, wanting to get to know her better.

"No, they live right outside of Miami. That's where I grew up."

"How did you end up in Key West?"

"Friends moved there, so I followed. My parents weren't too keen on the idea because they wanted me to stay home, go to college, get a degree, and then maybe get married and have babies," Ella laughed. "But they are fine with it now. Especially since they've seen how hard I've worked to get to where I am. Plus, I did it on my own."

"They must be proud," Tanner said, taking his and Ella's plates to the sink.

"I guess so."

"So, my next question is why?"

Ella looked at him puzzled. "Why what?"

"Why would you leave a tropical beach for a snowstorm?"

"I think you know the answer to that question. It might be warmer in the Keys, but this is nice and cozy too. It's a whole new world up here, and I really like it. Except my feet are still cold with two pair of socks on."

"Then let's go sit by the fireplace," Tanner said.

"Actually, that sounds like a great idea, but I need to clean this kitchen up first. I don't know what time Seth will be here in the morning."

"Not sure if he will get here that soon, but I'll help you get this cleaned up."

Soon, Ella and Tanner were sitting by the fire. Ella stretched her feet as close to the warmth as she could and finally felt like her feet were back home on her tropical island.

"Would you like some wine?" Tanner asked.

"That does sound good. Seth actually has some here?"

"Yes, I know where the secret stash is," Tanner said quickly.

"So he has wine but not much food?" Ella grinned.

"You have to have the right priorities," Tanner laughed as he headed out of the room.

It wasn't long before he was back on the couch, setting two wine glasses and the bottle of white on the table beside the sofa. Once he handed her the glass and he had his, he leaned back and relaxed as best as he could. It was difficult, with Ella being so close. As the minutes ticked by, the physical attraction he felt toward this woman grew. He knew he should leave and go into the other room, but he couldn't help it. He wanted to be there with her.

"So, tell me more about Key West."

"I've already told you mostly everything. Besides, I'm sure Seth has filled you in too after his trip."

"Just that next time, he wanted me to go because he said I would love it." Seth had also told him that he would love the women there, but Tanner purposely left that part out.

"You probably would, but you seem awfully at home here. You like working on the ranch, don't you?"

"I do, but sometimes, I wonder if there is something else I should be doing. I've been here all my life, and there are times I just want to go explore."

"That's how I felt before I left Miami, though I'm only three hours from home," Ella said. "It was hard at first, but I'm glad I did it. Don't get me wrong - I miss my parents and sister terribly, but I've made a good life in Key West."

Ella yawned. Between the excitement of her trip and now a full stomach, she was tired. Her long day was catching up with her, plus the coziness of the ranch house made her feel secure. "I think it's time for me to go to bed. Getting awfully sleepy."

They both stood up. Tanner was standing so close, he could smell the scent from Ella's hair, probably from the floral shampoo he imagined her using on her dark tresses. It would be so easy for him to just reach over and kiss her, but thankfully, Ella moved, making her way toward her room.

"Tanner, thank you so much for everything today. Seth has a really good friend in you. Goodnight," Ella said, then went up the stairs and out of sight.

Tanner sat back down on the couch, taking a sip of his wine while staring into the flames leaping in the fireplace. Was he really a good friend? Right now, he wanted to intimately know the girl upstairs, and that wasn't a good thing. Ella was here for Seth. But there was just something about her that was driving him a bit crazy. She was as close to perfection as he could imagine in a woman. He saw why Seth was so enamored by the island girl.

11

Ella felt as though she was in a fog, with a faint buzzing sound in the distance. When she first opened her eyes, she was slightly disoriented but soon realized where she was. The bed was so warm as she snuggled under the pile of blankets that had been left at the foot of her bed. Ella didn't want to reach for the ringing device but finally did, only to feel cold air on her skin. She grabbed her phone and was soon back under the covers. With one look at the phone screen, she found herself grinning. It was Seth.

"Good morning," Ella said, her voice still sounding sleepy.

"Good morning to you. Did I wake you up?" Seth said quickly.

"It's okay. Anyone else, and I wouldn't have answered the phone," Ella said with a little laugh. "What time is it?"

"It's a little after ten o'clock, your time, but eight o'clock there. I figured you would still be on Eastern Time, so that is why I called."

"I guess I had such a long day yesterday. Then Tanner and I stayed up after dinner and talked."

"Tanner? He's there with you? All night?" Seth tried not to sound shocked by her revelation, but he was sure his voice probably gave him away.

"The snow was coming down so heavy, it created something... I forgot what he called it. Anyway, his dad called and told him to stay put. Charlie said earlier that you sometimes let people sleep here, so I didn't think it would be a problem. Your friend is a really nice guy."

He sure is, Seth thought. More than you know!

Seth hated to think this way about his best friend, but in the past, he had always joked about Tanner's way with women. Girls seemed to flock to Tanner, and he loved every minute. Tanner had probably had more girlfriends that all the men on the ranch combined, but the two of them were still best friends. Seth would watch how women would be so attracted to Tanner and wonder why. It never bothered him until this yesterday, and now, this revelation. Things were different. Tanner was with Ella. Would he work his charms on her?

"Yeah, he is nice. We've been friends for quite a while."

"I know. He told me some very funny stories about you two while we were sitting in front of the fireplace, sipping on some wine. That was the one thing you did have in your kitchen." Ella laughed at the words, but Seth knew she was just about right.

They had wine together? In front of the fireplace? Those were things I wanted to do with her, Seth thought, jealousy rearing its ugly head. He had never felt this way before. It confused him but also let him know that Ella meant much more to him than he previously thought.

"Seth, are you there?"

Hearing Ella's voice brought Seth back to the present. He was not going to let this piece of news ruin his day. He would be back there today, somehow, some way.

"I'm here. Sorry, just a lot of noise here."

"Are you still in Atlanta? Will you be here today?" Ella asked.

"My flight was supposed to leave at six a.m. but was delayed due to the snow. We are hoping to leave around eleven o'clock. Are you doing okay?" Seth asked.

"I'm fine. Just wish you were here. I can't wait for you to show me around. But I have to admit I'm not sure about this cold. It was hard to reach out from beneath the covers to get the phone because it's cold in here, but I'm glad I did."

"Isn't the heater running? You should be really warm," Seth said concerned.

"It is. But I'm used to hot weather. I might end up layering every bit of clothing I brought with me to keep warm," Ella said with a laugh.

Seth pictured that sight, and even though it might look goofy, to Seth, it actually seemed sexy. Ella was beautiful no matter what, and just hearing her voice made him wish that he was already in the air, on his way to her.

"I'll be right there," Ella said loudly.

"What was that?"

"Tanner was just letting me know that he fixed breakfast. I think he said biscuits, eggs, and gravy. Didn't know he cooked."

"He usually doesn't," Seth said calmly. "He leaves that up to his mom. You must have really done some shopping yesterday."

"I did. Those cabinets were pretty bare, mister," Ella said. "Maybe when you get here, we can make those chocolate chip cookies you like so much. I made sure to buy the ingredients yesterday. With all this snow, it might be something fun we can do inside to stay warm."

Seth immediately imagined other ways to keep toasty, but they didn't involve a kitchen. "Sounds perfect," Seth said. "Ella, I can't wait to see you. I'm so sorry about this whole mix-up. I feel like I'm missing so much time with you."

"It's okay. We will have plenty of time together. And you are going to show me your little piece of Montana. But right now, I'm going to put on something warm and get my breakfast, and you're going to go hop on that plane. I'll see you soon!"

"I can't wait."

Seth stood there, digesting the conversation he had just had. Ella was having breakfast with Tanner. It should be him. If only he had called her to tell her he was coming to Key West, none of this would have happened. That eleven o'clock flight couldn't get here fast enough for him.

❊ ❊ ❊

"Hmm, that smells good," Ella said as she walked into the kitchen to find Tanner pulling a pan of biscuits from the oven. "You never said anything last night about cooking."

"I've learned a few things from my momma." Tanner smiled, and Ella was glad he was here. Even though she wished it was Seth, she loved having someone to talk to in this new place.

Tanner kept his cool, but seeing Ella had him excited. She looked absolutely adorable, with her dark hair pulled up into a messy bun and no make-up because she certainly didn't need any. She was bundled up in one of the sweatshirts she got yesterday and flannel pajama pants, with the thick socks she had also purchased during her shopping trip.

"Smells like something might be burning," Ella said, bringing Tanner's attention back to the breakfast cooking on the stove. But thankfully, it was just a bit of gravy that had dripped from the large spoon onto the back burner.

"I just got off the phone with Seth. He's leaving shortly for Seattle and then he says he should be able to get a flight here, but he's not sure when. This snowstorm really messed things up."

"Well, you two put the biggest wrinkle in the plan. Still can't believe you were both thinking the same thing," Tanner said as he made plates of food for the both of them.

"At least the snow is falling lighter. That means the worst of this storm is probably over. I checked, and the Great Falls Airport is open, so that is a good sign. Hopefully, Seth will be here tonight." As Tanner said the words, he had conflicting thoughts. This time alone with Ella was so nice. Probably better than any other woman he had been with, which, he admitted to himself, was a lot. He was a big flirt, but no one had really held his attention until Ella.

"Oh my gosh! This is so good. I feel like I'm home. There is this restaurant in Key West that makes wonderful biscuits and gravy, but this might just have them beat," Ella said, even though her mouth was full.

"I guess I've been paying better attention to how my mom cooks more than I thought. But then again, biscuits and gravy is a staple around the house."

"Do you still live with your parents?"

"No, I have my own place. Not like this," Tanner said, gesturing around at Seth's house, "but a small place closer to town. Perfect for just me."

"So, no one special in your life right now?" Ella asked.

Tanner almost didn't know what to say. Would you be my special someone? he thought to himself, then couldn't believe he thought the words. This was Seth's girl, and he had to keep that in mind. But if Seth made one wrong move, he would sweep in and do what he could to keep Ella for himself.

"No, just me at the moment."

"That's hard to believe. Super nice, took me shopping, good-looking, and can cook? You have got to be a catch around here."

Damn, why did she have to be so amazing? Tanner thought but didn't voice the words.

"Thank you for the compliments, but I just haven't found the right girl yet."

"Well, when you do, she will be very lucky."

Tanner needed to change the subject quickly. "So, since we have the whole day, anything special you'd like to do? I'm sure that I can get out of work today."

Ella sat for a second, looking around. "What is there to do, and how can you get out of work so easily?"

"I kind of know the boss," Tanner said with a grin. "It is still snowing outside but just lightly. Should stop in a few hours. Then we could go for a walk, a ride on the snowmobiles, or even go horseback riding."

"Or we could stay inside, where it's nice and warm," Ella said with a slight laugh.

"That too. You like board games?"

"Most definitely! My sister and I were Monopoly champs."

"Not sure if Seth has a Monopoly board around, but I'll have to check. We keep stuff like that here because we sometimes lose Wi-Fi, so the Internet can be spotty, especially when we have weather like we have now."

"How about some poker?" Ella asked.

"Now, you're talking." Tanner now sat down with his plate and had to admit that he had cooked a good meal. Or he was just starving. But from the look of Ella's plate, almost devoid of food, she had liked his cooking too.

Tanner noticed that Ella was looking out the window with a faraway gaze.

"Whatcha thinking?" Tanner asked before taking a big bite of eggs.

Ella looked at Tanner. She didn't want to hurt his feelings. He had been so helpful since she had arrived, but she wished so much that she was having this breakfast with Seth. She wished that she was planning a day with Seth instead. And hopefully, she would be this evening. She could only pray that the planes would be flying once again today.

"Just watching the snowfall outside. You're right. Not as thick as before. Last night reminded me of the huge downpours we have at home, like a tropical storm but icy."

"Yeah, I guess they are similar. Never been through a storm like that but have watched them on the TV. Seems like they can get a little intense."

"They can be, especially when you're on a little island. But thank goodness, they don't come too often. From the way you and your father talked yesterday, snowstorms must be more frequent."

"They can be. Last night's storm was just a bit stronger than usual. See? You came at just the right time. Now, there is more snow to go play in," Tanner said, smiling at her.

Ella wanted to agree, but her trip wasn't turning out like she had envisioned. Seth wasn't there.

12

Seth stretched once more, having slept only off and on during the night. But the announcement he heard was music to his ears. His eleven o'clock flight would be able to leave after all. The planes were flying again, and he might finally get home. Get to Ella.

Seth wanted to call once more before getting on the plane, but he didn't have time. He still couldn't get over the fact that Tanner had spent the night and was now cooking breakfast for her! Seth only hoped that Tanner had kept his distance during the night.

One look out the airport windows made him smile. It was nice here in Atlanta, and he kept his fingers crossed that the flight would be smooth all the way to Seattle. Then that his flight to Great Falls would be available. If so, he would be with Ella late this afternoon.

As he stood in line to board the plane, he heard his phone buzz a notification sound. One look at the screen made him smile. "I miss you" was all it said, and it was from Ella. As soon as he was sitting in his seat, he quickly texted her back: "I miss you too". At least he knew she was thinking about him, even though she was with Tanner.

He wanted to continue their conversation through texting, but soon, he heard the announcement to turn off all electronic devices, so Seth decided to just sit back and try to get some sleep. Though he had gotten some rest the night before, it hadn't been as comfortable as the first class seat he was in now.

But just the thought of being one step closer to Ella brought a smile to his face. He was excited to get home. He had so much he wanted to share with her, and even though he would have to show her some of his favorite places in a shorter amount of time, that was okay. Even if they did nothing but stay at the house, that would be fine with him. Seth couldn't wait to talk to her, be with her. Just knowing that she had made the surprise visit meant so much to him.

"The snow has stopped," Ella said, looking through the window beside the fireplace. It was stunning outside. Though it was still cloudy overhead, the scene before her was magical. The snow was fresh now, with no footprints or tire marks. With the slope of the land and the mountains in the distance, it was something she had only dreamed of before. And with the crackling of the fireplace beside her, Ella almost felt like she had been dropped into a movie set.

"Hopefully, we will have sunshine this afternoon. I say we go riding on the snowmobiles this afternoon," Tanner said, coming to stand beside her, gazing out the window.

"Hopefully, we'll have to pick up Seth."

"Oh, we'll have plenty of time," Tanner said. The thought of her riding behind him on the machine was so enticing. He imagined her arms wrapped around his waist. He knew he was treading on dangerous ground, but he couldn't help it. Plus, Tanner rationalized in his mind that riding the horses today probably wasn't a good idea after such a heavy snow last night.

"Sounds like fun. Then what do you want to do this morning?" Ella said.

Tanner's mind went to things he shouldn't even be thinking about, but he quickly pushed the thoughts away as much as he could. "Well, you mentioned poker, or I could take you for a ride around the ranch, to show you how things are done around here. That way, most of time, you will be in a nice, warm truck."

"I opt for the ride around the ranch. It would give me the opportunity to take some great pictures of all this snow! I can't wait to show my family, though they don't know I'm here," Ella said, her voice going from complete enthusiasm to wistfulness.

"You didn't tell then you were coming to Montana?"

"No. I think they would have talked me out of it."

"Do they know about Seth?"

"I told my mom that I met a guy a few months ago, but that's about it. They know I'm pretty focused on school right now, so she didn't ask me any questions."

"Well, go put your new clothes on. It's a bit nippy out there, and you'll need all that stuff you bought."

"I need to wear it all?" Ella asked, surprised.

"No," Tanner laughed. "I didn't mean it all. Just make sure to dress warmly and include your hat, scarf, and gloves. Plus, your boots. It's only five degrees outside. Don't want you getting frost-bite."

"Sorry," Ella said. "You gotta remember I'm used to flip-flops and shorts. This is all new to me."

"I hope I didn't come across condescending. I surely didn't mean it like that. I just know that you've never experienced this kind of weather. Want to make sure you'll be warm."

"Then I'll be right back," Ella said, practically racing to her room.

Tanner hoped that he was doing the right thing. He was sure that Seth wanted to show her the ranch, but Tanner knew that if he stayed much longer with her in this house, he was sure to lose it. And he didn't want to leave her alone all day, though he was sure she would be okay. He honestly hadn't been so attracted to a woman in his entire life. Or it sure felt like it right now, and he didn't want to lose what willpower he had in this situation.

"That was quick," Tanner said as Ella popped back into the room, dressed with so many of her clothes that Tanner could only make out the beautiful brown eyes peering over the scarf and her dark hair flowing from underneath the hat.

"Will this do?" Ella asked, her voice muffled by the scarf.

"You look perfect," Tanner said, and he meant that in more ways than one.

Seth didn't realize how tired he was till the flight attendant gently shook him awake.

"Sir, we are about an hour outside of Seattle. Hate to wake you, but thought you might want to know."

"Have you heard about the weather? Are flights going to Great Falls or to the upper Midwest?"

"I'm not sure, but someone should be able to help you at the gate, when you get inside the terminal." The young lady smiled and then helped the older lady behind him.

As Seth looked out the window, the skies were cloudy, but he had seen worse before. He could only keep his fingers crossed that he would get good news as soon as he landed.

Soon, Seth was standing in the line with many others, hoping to get connecting flights to various destinations that had been delayed due to the winter weather. When it was his turn, and after he talked to the counter agent, he was so happy, he about jumped over the desk to give the man a hug. There was a flight to Great Falls in just one hour. With his ticket in hand, he raced to the boarding gate.

Seth was just about to dial Ella's number when an idea came to mind. Instead, he selected Charlie's number.

"Nice to hear from you today, boss. Where you at now?" Charlie asked.

"I'm finally in Seattle, and I have a plane that is leaving shortly. I'll be in Great Falls in two hours. Don't tell anyone. I want to surprise Ella because I told her I didn't know when I would be there. Can you pick me up, if everything is okay at the ranch?"

"What is it with you and surprises lately? Haven't you learned your lesson, young man?" Charlie chuckled. "Sure. You know I'll be there. And the ranch is fine. I'll see you in a bit."

Seth was excited now. He couldn't wait to see the look on Ella's face when he showed up. He was going to be able to surprise her after all. Then he would give her the gift he had taken all the way to the Keys with him. It was a white gold horse. He had brought it to give to her as a reminder of him once he left to go home. But now that she was in Montana, he didn't want her to leave.

Seth found himself yet again in another plane, but this time, this plane was taking him home. So, he sat back and relaxed as the plane lifted off into the air. The ride was a bit bumpy at first, with the weather that had passed through, but before he knew it, they were above the clouds, and bright sunshine filled the plane.

He hoped it would be sunny when he arrived at the ranch because it was always beautiful after a snowfall. He just hoped Ella liked it as much as he did.

13

As they drove around the ranch, Ella couldn't get over the size of it. Seth had shown her pictures when he was in Key West, and she had looked up ranches on the Internet before her trip, but this was nowhere near what she had expected. There were huge buildings, cattle that seemed to be everywhere, and horses too. Even though it had snowed heavily the previous night, the animals were outside.

"I can't believe those animals aren't frozen," Ella said as they slowly drove past the herd.

"No, we take care to keep them sheltered. We use those buildings," Tanner said, pointing to the large structures in the distance, "and we have covered areas. We make sure to have lots of feed and water available. The ones we worry about the most are the expectant mommas. We really have to watch out for them."

"I can't imagine an animal being able to survive out here. I'm covered from head to toe and still cold."

"I can turn up the heater a bit more," Tanner said, reaching for the knob on the dash.

"Thanks. I promise I'll get warm shortly. I thought I had put on enough clothes this time."

"Maybe since you are a southern girl, you just might have to wear most of your wardrobe when you are out and about," Tanner said with a laugh.

Ella silently agreed with him. He was probably right. She had never been so cold in her life, but at the same time, she loved every minute of being on the ranch. Except for the fact that Seth wasn't here. But she would see him tonight, and she couldn't wait.

"Not sure if we should go out in the snow mobiles if you are this cold," Tanner said. They turned right, toward another large building, but nothing as big as the others they had seen around the ranch.

"I think I'll be okay. It will be fun. Once again, I've heard about them but never been on one. I've seen them in the movies, though. Reminded me of jet skis on snow."

"Never thought of it that way, but I guess it's similar. You sure did a lot of research before coming up here, didn't you?"

"I had to. If I was going to surprise Seth, I needed to know what to expect. I thought I was prepared, but now, I can say not so much. Thank you for all the help. It means a lot."

"You're more than welcome." Tanner parked in front of the building and was around to her side of the truck just as she slid out of the seatbelt. "Well, let's go give this a shot. Just promise me a few things."

"What's that?" Ella asked, perplexed.

"That you will hold on to me tight. Can't have you flying off the back of the snowmobile. Seth will have my head if you get hurt."

"I can do that, but what is the other?"

"If you get too cold, you will let me know. Seriously, I don't want you to get frostbite just because you want to see things and take pictures. Once again, I don't need Seth pissed at me."

"I promise I'll let you know. Now, where is the snowmobile?"

"Just come with me." Tanner reached out his hand, and Ella took it, not thinking anything about it. But for Tanner, it was a different story. The feel of her tiny hand in his was electrifying, and he couldn't wait to take her through the snow on the machine waiting in the huge garage.

❄ ❄ ❄

"Glad you're back," Charlie said as they both entered Seth's house.

"Me too." Seth set his bags down, looking around. He hoped that Ella would appear, but the house was quiet.

"You told me not to say anything so they aren't here," Charlie said as he noticed Seth looking from room to room.

"Where are they?" Seth said anxiously.

"Tanner was going to take her around the ranch, then maybe for a ride on the snowmobile. I know you probably wanted to do that, but I didn't want her to just sit here. Plus, you can take her horseback riding."

"No, it's okay. I wouldn't want her to be bored either," Seth said, thinking about how Tanner was with her, sharing experiences with Ella that were so different from her home in the Keys.

"Seems to be a pretty special gal," Charlie said, coming up to Seth and putting his hand on his shoulder. "By the way, both of you are invited to dinner tonight. Mary is back and is fixing my favorite: chili."

"I told Ella if I got back in time that we would go into town to eat tonight. Maybe we could take a rain check? I sure would love for her to meet Mary before she goes back to Florida." When Seth spoke of Ella returning to the Keys, he felt disappointment creeping though him. Just the thought of Ella going back home wasn't sitting well with him, and he hadn't even seen her yet! Maybe that was part of the problem.

"Completely understand. To tell you the truth, if I were in your shoes, I would want her all to myself tonight too. Let's plan on dinner tomorrow, then, okay?" Charlie asked.

"Sounds great. I'll ask Ella, but I'm sure she will be okay with it too."

"I think Mary just wants to meet this girl that has stolen your heart and made you act so nutty."

"I'm not that bad," Seth said. He turned to look at Charlie, who clearly looked back at him like he was not in his right mind. "She is just a special friend."

"Special friend, my ass! Seth, I've known you for a long time, son, and I've never seen you like this. Now, Tanner, on the other hand, seems to have a new girlfriend every week, which drives his momma up a tree. Where that boy learned to flirt is beyond me."

Seth listened to Charlie's words and imagined what Tanner was up to right now. Was he flirting with Ella? Had he been inappropriate with her at all? Ella was a woman that could definitely take care of herself, but she was also polite and probably wouldn't say anything if Tanner did.

"Seth, did you hear me?"

"I'm sorry. I was just thinking about things I need to do since Ella's not here now. What did you say?"

"I told you to act as though you were still off on your little vacation. I've got everything taken care of around here. But there was a new calf born yesterday, during that snowstorm, and I need to go check on things. Tracey has already given it a name."

"She gives every new calf a name. What is it this time?" Seth wondered because Tracey, one of their female ranch hands, always named every new calf, though they all eventually forgot their names.

"Snowshoe."

"Snowshoe?" Seth asked, eyebrows furrowed.

"Yeah, because she had to put on her snowshoes just to get to the barn yesterday. That snow was thick. Couldn't see your hand in front of your face."

"You'd never know it today, except for the high drifts. I'm just glad it was a quick storm."

"I'm glad for you too. But I gotta go. Also meeting that new boy we just hired. He is a little greener around a ranch than he let on. But I still think he'll work out. Just gonna need a bit more training. I'll make sure Tanner is on it first thing tomorrow."

"Thanks, Charlie. I'm going to go unpack and get a shower before Ella and Tanner return."

"And I need to get this truck out of here, so they don't suspect anything. Good luck with your surprise," Charlie said, smiling at Seth before walking out the door.

The house looked as it did when he left it but with some food on the kitchen counter. He walked to his bedroom, but not before peeking in the room he had told Charlie to prepare for Ella. That was her stuff, all right, along with the scent of Ella's perfume. She was really here. He knew that she was, but to finally be able to see her after these last two days of mix-ups was so exciting. But right now, he needed a shower.

* * *

"Oh my gosh!" Ella exclaimed. "That was so much fun! And it did remind me a bit of the jet skis but smoother. No waves to jump over." Ella climbed off the back of the snowmobile, took off her helmet, and shook out her hair.

Once again, Tanner couldn't help but be enchanted by her. She saw beauty and fun in everything. Things that he took for granted, Ella thought were fascinating. But then he might feel the same way if he were down in the Keys. In her part of the country.

"Maybe when Seth gets back, the two of you can go again. Maybe next time, you can drive. I just thought it would be better to let me steer today since we had so much snow yesterday."

Plus, having your arms around me was a treat, Tanner thought to himself.

"Oh, no! I think I'm a better passenger than driver. But I'll definitely make Seth take me out again. Maybe you could come with us. Bring someone with you."

Ella had no idea how her simple remark was affecting Tanner. If Seth wasn't his best friend, it wouldn't matter who Ella thought she liked. Tanner would be doing whatever he could to woo this girl.

Last night, as he slept on the couch, all he could think about was the beauty in the upstairs room. Normally, he wasn't one to sleep alone, but this was different. He was just taking care of Ella till Seth returned, which he hoped was soon because being with Ella all day was a bit much for him. She was intoxicating.

As soon as he woke this morning, Tanner couldn't wait to see her. He fixed breakfast, hoping the smell would wake her and cause her to come down, and he wasn't disappointed. Then today, riding over the snow, her sitting behind him with her arms wrapped securely around his waist sent a wave of desire through him so strong that he couldn't believe what was happening. Whatever magic spell Ella possessed, she had worked its magic on him.

"I think by the time Seth gets home, you two are going to want some time to yourself. You didn't travel all the way up here to see me or my dad."

"I just hope Seth feels the same way," Ella said softly.

"Are you kidding? He just went all the way to Key West to see you. That should give you the answer you are looking for."

Tanner saw the blush staining Ella's cheeks, and it wasn't from the cold ride they just finished. She really cared for Seth, and Tanner was truly happy for the two of them. But he still couldn't help himself for being so attracted to her.

"Let's make our way back to the house. It won't be long before we need to head to the airport to pick up Seth."

"I can't believe he will be here today. Finally," Ella said, jumping up and down just for a second.

But as she turned to grab the door handle of the truck, she stepped into the snow but found a deep hole instead. As she tried to steady herself, she put her other foot down, only to be met with a patch of ice. Before she knew it, she was on the snow-covered ground, but her landing wasn't graceful or painless. She felt the shooting pain suddenly traveling up her leg from her foot, and the side of her head was throbbing. She felt like she couldn't move.

"Ella!"

Ella heard the voice and knew it was Tanner but felt slightly dazed. She never thought a hole would be hiding under the snow, nor she did she know why her head was suddenly hurting so bad.

"Where are you hurt?" Tanner asked, suddenly at her side, propping her up in his arms. But one look at her face and the amount of blood dripping down her cheek let Tanner know she had taken a bad fall.

"My right ankle and foot hurt bad. And my head."

Tanner saw where she had stepped and knew that it was much deeper than it should have been. A hole. Probably from one of the dogs.

"I think you hit the side of the truck when you fell. You have a nice cut and are bleeding pretty good. I need to get you to a doctor. You may have broken your foot too."

"No, I'll be fine. Let's just get to the house, so I can get cleaned up."

Ella tried to stand and felt a little dizzy. Plus, the pain radiating from her foot almost took her breath away.

"Give me just a sec," Ella said, trying to sit back in the snow.

"Just put your arms around my neck. I've got you," Tanner said.

Before Ella knew what was happening, Tanner had her cradled in his arms, and she dutifully did as he had asked. The way she felt at the moment, she needed all the support she could get. Part of her was frustrated over her silly accident because she wanted everything to be perfect for when Seth arrived. But then she was hurting so badly, couldn't walk, and her head was throbbing. It was hard to think straight.

"I'm going to take you to Dr. Walker. Or better yet, I'll call him and get him to come to Seth's house."

"Doctors make house calls around here?" Ella asked.

"Well, he is the resident vet here on the ranch, but he takes care of us too, unless it's something major and then he sends us on to the doc in town. Have a feeling that's what he going to say about you, but I'll call and have him meet us at the house."

Ella didn't disagree this time. Something was definitely up with her foot, and she reached up to her face, only to come away with blood covering her hand.

"I've got to get cleaned up before we go pick up Seth."

"Ella, that is the last thing you need to worry about right now. Just sit tight, and I'll have you back to the house in no time."

Tanner made sure Ella was strapped in and saw the cut was bleeding heavier now. He found a napkin in the truck, gave it to her, and told her to keep pressure on it till she got to the house. As he looked at her, Tanner hoped that Seth wouldn't be too upset. He had promised his dad that he would keep Ella safe today, and now, she looked like she had been in a bad accident, not just a step in a hole hidden under the snow.

Tanner made the call to the doctor as he drove carefully back to the house, trying not to jar the truck too much. He felt relieved when they were finally parked in front of the house.

"The doctor is on his way, and we need to get you in the house. Don't move till I come over there," Tanner said. Ella could only nod.

She didn't want to sound like a baby, but her foot hurt terribly, plus she was so tired. When Tanner opened the door and proceeded to scoop her in his arms again, she didn't complain. She wrapped her arms around him, placing her head on his chest. She was tired and hurting.

"Ella, don't go to sleep. The doctor said you might have a concussion. So, keep talking to me, okay?" Tanner said.

"I'm fine, really," Ella said, then yawned.

"Just about inside."

"Sounds good," Ella murmured. She snuggled into Tanner's chest, unaware that Seth was watching from the upstairs window as the scene outside unfolded.

14

Seth knew it. Tanner might be his best friend – or at least he used to be – but he had done just what Seth had suspected. As he watched him carry Ella up the sidewalk and saw the girl he was falling in love with snuggled into his friend's chest, Seth's heart sank.

How does Tanner do that? Seth thought. He had only been with Ella for two days, and the girl he thought was his seemed to be cozy with his best friend.

Seth didn't make it down the steps before Tanner was in the front door, with Ella still in his arms. Seth stood on the inside steps, and neither Tanner nor Ella saw him. He watched for a few moments as Tanner gently laid Ella on the couch, hovering over her so close, he was sure they were kissing.

"Surprise," Seth said nonchalantly as he took the last steps to his living room.

"Seth?" Ella asked, not able to see him, but she clearly heard his voice.

Tanner's head jerked up suddenly. "Seth, you're here! How? Thought you were coming in later this afternoon!"

"I can see that." Seth felt crushed because Ella didn't even get up from the couch to see him. She just continued to lie where she was, saying his name with no excitement whatsoever. Now, he wasn't sure he wanted to face her. He had fought his way back to Montana just to be with her, and Ella had turned on him. And with his friend!

"Listen, stay here with Ella, and I'll go watch for the doctor. He should be here any minute." Tanner stood, turned, and was almost out the door before Seth could reach the couch.

Seth immediately felt like he had stepped into another reality. Upon seeing Ella, he saw the blood now having dripped down the side of her face, matting her hair near the top of her forehead. Then he noticed that she had one boot on, but the other was nowhere to be seen. And she looked like she was sleeping.

"Ella? What happened?" Seth said, immediately kneeling on the floor beside the couch. He took the napkin out of her hand, trying to wash away some of the blood, but it was beginning to dry. He only wished she would wake up.

"Ella? Wake up, sweetheart," Seth said soothingly, and her eyes fluttered open.

"You're finally here," Ella said sleepily.

"What happened?"

"I fell. Silly of me," Ella said softly, her eyes closing again.

"Ella, tell me what happened." Seth knew he had to keep her awake. She fell, and with the gash on her head, he put it all together that she could have a concussion. Maybe what he saw outside the window only moments ago wasn't what he thought. Seth suddenly felt like a jerk, but he would address that later. Ella was the most important thing right now. If she was attracted to Tanner, Seth couldn't think about it at the moment.

Seth heard the door open and looked up to see Dr. Walker and Tanner come in the house. He moved out of the way and watched as the doctor assessed Ella.

"She stepped into a hole. Twisted her foot pretty badly and fell against the truck when she tried to catch herself. She also slid on the ice." Seth listened as Tanner recounted what happened and closed his eyes. He should have been there to protect her. She wasn't used to this.

"Ella, I need you to talk to me," Dr. Walker said. "Can you do that?"

"Sure." Ella's eyes opened but then immediately shut again.

"I'm pretty sure she has a concussion. Nothing I haven't seen you boys do around here, but to be safe, I think she needs to been seen by Roger in town. I'll give him a call and let him know you'll be there shortly. Plus, she needs that foot X-rayed. Probably just a bad sprain, but it's swelling pretty good. If it's broken, she'll need a cast."

"I'll get the truck warmed up," Tanner said quickly.

"No, I'll take her," Seth replied, looking stoically at his friend.

"I suggest you both take her. Let Tanner drive, and you," Dr. Walker said, looking at Seth, "make sure she stays awake. Keep her talking. I know she wants to sleep, but she needs to be awake. She's gonna be okay. But get going."

This time, it was Seth who gently picked up Ella off the couch. Her eyes fluttered opened and she smiled.

"Hey, beautiful. I need you to stay awake for me, okay?" Seth said as he walked to the truck where Tanner was already waiting.

"I'm so glad you're finally here," Ella said softly. "Sorry about all of this. It seems this idea of mine isn't working out quite like I planned."

Seth laughed. "I think we could both say that."

"Tanner has been wonderful. He's a really nice guy."

Seth couldn't help the feeling of jealousy that rose up inside of him at the mention of Tanner's name. He thought that now he had Ella in his arms, Tanner would no longer be a part of this equation. But they had spent a fair amount of time together. Seth only hoped that Ella's original intention for coming to Montana was still the same: to spend time with him. And he hoped that

Tanner hadn't worked his way into her mind, making her think twice about her choices. But right now, Seth had to stay calm for Ella's sake.

"Yes, he is. But you got hurt while you were with him."

"Oh, it was my fault. Not use to this snow and ice. Can't see holes in the ground when they are covered with all this pretty white stuff."

Seth was glad she was talking, but one look at her face, and it seemed as though she could easily fall asleep. Her eyes looked drowsy, and she was relaxed in his arms. But they were at the truck.

Seth knew that Ella would be sitting between him and Tanner, and that made him a bit uncomfortable, but at the same time, glad that he had someone to help him. He gently put Ella on the seat, then helped her scoot to the middle. Tanner reached out and put his arms around her to help, and Seth wanted to tell him to back off, but he realized that Tanner was only helping. Right now, Seth had to think about what was best for Ella. He would confront his feelings about Tanner later.

The drive to town seemed to take forever. Tanner recounted again what happened, and Ella filled in some details too. Seth was glad that she was talking, and she seemed a bit more aware. That gave him hope that her injuries weren't serious, though her foot was swelling larger by the minute.

The town doctor was waiting on them as soon as they pulled up. Seth was quick to make sure that Ella was in his arms, not Tanner's, and took her into the office. But it was only minutes before she was whisked away behind the double doors to the back, where the exam rooms were. Seth and Tanner watched her till she was out of their sight, then took seats across from each other in the waiting room.

The silence between the two men seem to last only seconds before the words came tumbling out of Seth. "How could you let this happen?"

"What do you mean 'let this happen'? I didn't know that hole was there. Stuff like this goes on every day around the ranch."

Seth knew Tanner was right, but he still felt angry that Ella was hurt. And in his mind, it was Tanner's fault.

"She's not used to ranch life. You should have been there."

"Geez, Seth, I was there. It was just an accident. Could've happened to any of us. She's a tough girl. She's gonna be fine," Tanner said.

"Tough girl? How would you know?" Seth said a bit louder than he should.

"What's wrong with you?"

Seth ran his fingers through his hair, feeling intense anger for the man sitting across from him. He wanted to punch Tanner. Though Ella was hurt and everything Tanner said was true, he still felt like there was something between Ella and Tanner that he didn't know about just yet. It felt like something special had slipped through his fingers.

"Just worried, okay?"

"Seth, she's gonna be fine. Just relax."

"Relax? When I see you carrying the girl I love in the house, her all cradled in your arms? I know you, Tanner. You have a way to get women to do anything, and you probably took advantage of Ella's..."

"Are you serious? Really? And you want to talk about this here, at the doctor's office, while Ella's being looked at?"

Seth couldn't think straight. Maybe it was a combination of little sleep, the events of the last two days, and just knowing his friend's usual behavior around women.

"I just know you, Tanner. Wouldn't surprise me if you made a play for her."

"Glad to know that you think so highly of me," Tanner said sarcastically and rolled his eyes. "Man, you know I wouldn't do that."

"I've seen you over the years. You could teach the Pope to flirt! Every guy on the ranch wants to be with you when we go out because you know how to attract the women. Now, you've spent the last two days with Ella? What am I supposed to think?" Seth's cheeks were now hot, and he knew that his blood pressure was probably through the roof.

"You make me sound like I'm a predator. I can't help it all the girls like me," Tanner said with a laugh, but for Seth, it didn't lighten the mood. "Come on, Seth. I didn't know you had no trust in me. And you have to admit, not all the girls like me." Seth knew Tanner was trying to defuse the tension, but it wasn't working.

Seth just sat there and stared at his friend for a few seconds before standing up and walking toward the closed door, where the doctor had taken Ella. He wanted to be back there with her so badly and make sure that everything was all right.

"You know, I can't believe you," Tanner said, now standing right behind Seth.

"Let's see. You've had how many girlfriends just this year?" Seth said, the anger in his voice dripping with every word.

"You really want to do this here?"

Seth looked around the waiting room to see that all eyes were on them. But before Seth could answer Tanner's question, the doctor came through the door, almost hitting both men.

"You two know by now that we do have seats in the waiting room," the doctor said.

"Sorry," they both said in unison.

"How is she?" Seth asked.

"She is going to be okay. Did some X-rays. She has a bump on her head around the cut but no concussion. She was back there talking up a storm, and from the story she told me, I think she was tired from this crazy trip of hers. And yours, Seth, if what she told me is correct." The doctor chuckled just a bit.

"What about her foot?"

"Severe sprain – no broken bones. I was sure there were going to be a few fractures, but she is lucky. Though, she is going to have to stay off the foot for at least a week. Those tendons and ligaments are mighty angry with her right now. I'll wrap it up and put her in a boot cast to be on the safe side. She needs to keep it propped up and put no weight on it at all. She said she was flying back to Key West in a few days, and I advised against it. As long as her flights will take, she doesn't need to be in an airplane. Plus, I don't think she would be able to get around the airport with luggage and crutches."

"At least we have a few days to figure it out," Seth said. "When can she go home?"

"They are wrapping her foot now. We used steri-strips on the cut. Shouldn't have a bad scar. But she needs to keep that foot wrapped and propped up as much as possible, okay? Where is she staying?"

"Seth's house," Tanner answered quickly.

"Then you are responsible for her care," the doctor said, looking straight at Seth. "If you see any unusual swelling or she starts getting headaches and fatigue, bring her right back, okay?"

"Sure thing, Doc."

The doctor turned and walked back through the doors that led to the examining rooms. Seth went to sit back down, not saying a word to Tanner.

"Seth, seriously, don't do this, man. You know I wouldn't do anything like that to you."

Seth looked up at Tanner. "Then tell me you didn't have any thoughts about her. Nothing inappropriate? That nothing crossed your mind about wanting to be with her?"

Tanner was silent for just a few seconds and looked away. That was all the confirmation Seth needed to know what was in Tanner's mind.

"I knew it!" Seth said loudly.

"Hey, what's wrong?"

Seth and Tanner both turned to see Ella coming toward them in a wheelchair, with crutches across her lap.

"Nothing's wrong," Seth said, quickly smiling at her, then back to Tanner to hide what they had been fighting about.

"Just going over ranch stuff," Tanner replied, trying to play along, but he knew that his moment's hesitation had given him away. If only he could talk to Seth alone and explain his thoughts, he knew that Seth would understand that the situation wasn't what it appeared to be.

"Ready to go home?" Seth asked as he knelt before her.

"If you mean Key West, not quite yet. Now, as for the ranch, I'm more than ready to get back there."

"Then let's get you to the ranch." He leaned over and gave Ella a kiss on the forehead, then wheeled her out to Tanner's truck.

* * *

"I've got it," Seth said as Tanner tried to help him with Ella back at the house.

"I was just getting the door for you."

Seth just looked at his friend, trying to keep his conversation civil, but it was taking all Seth had to keep his words in check. He had been right all along. Tanner was interested in Ella, but if Seth had anything to do with it, Tanner wasn't coming near Ella at all.

"Thanks, but I think I have it."

Ella watched the exchange between the two men. Though she was drowsy from the medication given to her at the doctor's office, she had definitely noticed a tension-filled atmosphere in the truck on the ride back. The two men barely spoke to each other but asked her all kinds of questions.

Ella had no idea what was going on, but hopefully, Seth would fill in the details. Tanner had been nice and good to her, so she didn't like seeing both of them act this way. They were supposedly friends – best friends at that – and she couldn't think what could have happened to make them so tense.

Seth sat Ella down on the couch and then promptly propped her foot up.

"Seth, I promise, I can do things. You don't have to treat me like a china doll."

"You just had a bad fall, have a cut on your head, and a badly sprained foot. Let me take care of you."

Ella looked up at him and smiled. She had waited so long to see him, and now, here he was, right before her eyes. Though, she didn't think she would be in this kind of shape when he finally arrived back home. It was embarrassing to be almost helpless, but she was determined to make the most of her time here with Seth.

"I'm going to go now," Tanner said. "Ella, I'm really sorry about what happened today."

"It was just an accident, Tanner. I'm sure it could have happened to anyone."

"Maybe you can explain that to Seth." With those words, Tanner looked at her once more, then shut the front door.

"Seth, what is he talking about?" Ella looked over at the man sitting at her feet, gently propping her sprained foot up on a sofa pillow.

"Nothing, really," Seth answered, relieved that Tanner was finally gone.

"I don't believe that. You two barely talked to each other on the way home. And now, Tanner leaves on what seems to be a very sour note. Please tell me what's going on?"

"I promise it's no big deal. It's just been a long day for all of us. Right now, I want to spend some time with you," Seth said, pulling up the ottoman beside the couch where Ella was lying.

"And I want to spend every second with you till I have to go home. But you aren't going to keep this from me. My momma always told me I had a gift for knowing people and sensing things. Now, I know that there's something between you and Tanner you're keeping from me."

Seth reached over and stroked her face gently. "Can we talk about this in the morning? I've waited the last two days to see you. It's the only thing that kept me going through all the driving, sleeping in airports, and flying just to get back here as soon as I could. You can imagine what I thought when your boss told me you had left to come to Montana," Seth said, hoping to sidestep the conversation that he knew Ella would still demand that they have.

"Oh, yes, I can because I was stunned when I found out that you weren't here!" Ella answered his question, but she wasn't about to let go of the fact that she wanted to know what had happened between Tanner and Seth.

"I bet you were. How do you like all this snow?" Seth gestured toward the window, but Ella didn't look. "What's wrong?"

"I want to know what is going on between you and Tanner."

Seth sighed. She was stubborn, that was for sure, and he was having a hard time trying to find the right way to explain what had happened. About how he felt. But the look in Ella's eyes let him know that he had better start explaining himself.

15

"So, tell me." Ella's voice was soft and soothing, but Seth wasn't sure she would understand what he was thinking. He propped his elbows on his knees, leaning toward the couch, looking into the chocolate brown eyes he had been dreaming about the last two days.

"I'm just a little upset, that's all."

"At what? You mean with Tanner?" Ella asked.

"Yeah, just a bit frustrated."

"But why?"

How could he explain how he was feeling? Jealousy? Something he hadn't felt before in his life? It was an emotion that was truly foreign to him, but right now, it held him in a tight vice.

"Because he should have been more careful, so you wouldn't have gotten hurt. Now, it looks like you'll have to spend more time recuperating on this couch instead of me being able to show you my hometown, like you did with me when I was in Key West."

"But?"

"But what?" Seth asked, knowing that she could read between the lines.

"There is more, so you might as well go ahead and let me know what's going on between you two. You know I'll pester you till you tell me. Didn't you learn that when you were in the Keys?"

Seth was puzzled at first, wondering what she meant, but then he remembered their conversation over dinner one night. Ella had insisted on knowing about the conflict between his mother and father, especially since she had lived right next door to Seth's father's new wife, Josie. When Seth kept trying to change the subject, he remembered Ella would only look at him and smile with raised eyebrows, and Seth couldn't help but continue to answer her questions. She had a way to convince him to do things he had always been able to resist before.

"Tanner just has this way with women."

"So, what has that got to do with anything?"

"Well, you just spent two days with him. And I know he is feeling something for you."

Ella looked at him with eyes that seemed to want to pop and then she laughed.

"Me and Tanner? You can't be serious."

"I've seen him over the years, Ella. Even his dad, Charlie, said he never saw women flock to a man like they do Tanner."

Ella's expression changed. She didn't have that look of surprise or a smile on her face anymore.

"So, you think that I would just fall for some guy because other women are attracted to him? And that he could weave some magic spell over me that would have me falling at his feet?"

Seth heard a tiny hint of anger in Ella's voice and wished she could understand where he was coming from. "No, not really, but Tanner is..." Seth didn't get a chance to finish his sentence.

"I can't believe this. I came all this way to see you, Seth. And just because I had to spend some time with your friend doesn't mean I'm some easy chick that just falls for anyone. I thought you would know that by now. I know we haven't spent a lot of time together in person, but the phone calls and texts. Couldn't you tell that I might have a thing for you? Why else would I make this trip to Montana?"

Seth was speechless. He knew he had screwed up. Ella might not be feeling well, but he heard the fire in her voice.

"It's just that when I looked out the window when you and Tanner came home, I was excited about surprising you, and all I saw was you curled up in Tanner's arms," Seth exclaimed, hoping he was explaining himself correctly.

"I was hurt! Tanner was kind enough to carry me," Ella said, now sitting up, seeming to forget about her facial injury and her swollen foot.

"I know that now, but it's not what it looked like at the time."

"You just assumed the worse? Don't you have enough faith in me that you could have at least talked to me first, before thinking I'd taken up with your supposed best friend?"

The look that Ella was giving him made Seth feel like such a fool. She was right. He should have had enough faith in her that she would not have traveled all this way to see him if there was not more to their relationship.

"I think I need to go to bed," Ella said, trying to stand up. She landed back on the couch, flinching from the pain.

"Hey, where do you think you are going? It's early, and you need something to eat," Seth said, hoping the conversation would disappear.

"I'm tired and sleepy."

"And the doctor wanted you to stay awake for a while, just in case. What sounds good for dinner?" Seth asked as he sat back down on the ottoman right in front of Ella.

"Nothing."

"Ella, I know you're upset at me. I promise this wasn't how I planned this homecoming, and I'm sorry. But you have to eat something. How about a sandwich?" Seth talked soothingly to her, hoping to make things right. "Also, we've been invited over to Charlie's house tomorrow. Mary is cooking for us."

"Are you sure that a good idea? I mean, they're Tanner's parents. He might show up with his magical powers and sweep me away."

Seth hung his head. "Ella, I'm sorry. I don't know what else to say."

"Maybe this thing between you and me isn't what I thought it was," Ella said softly.

"But maybe it is. Just give me a chance. I just let overthinking get the best of me. And I'll work things out with Tanner, I promise."

"I guess I'll have to wait and see," Ella said, getting comfortable on the couch again.

* * *

The night before had been filled with tension. It was nothing that Ella had imagined once she saw Seth. She had been looking forward to the moment she would see him in Montana, and it seemed like everything had gone completely wrong.

When she woke this morning, she found herself still on Seth's couch, the fire still glowing in the stones in front of her. To her left, stretched out on the loveseat and ottoman, was Seth. She watched him as he slept, and even though she was still irritated about their conversation the night before, she couldn't help but feel happy that he was finally here. That she was seeing him in person after these months apart.

What really shocked her was that her desire for this man was stronger than she had thought, even with all the events of yesterday. This was more than a passing fancy. Though Seth had assumed some wrong thoughts about her and Tanner, she found herself feeling she was falling love with the sleeping man she couldn't help but watch.

They had eaten dinner last night, but their conversation had been very stifled. But then she was on pain medication, which made it hard to concentrate. The last thing she remembered before falling asleep was Seth pulling a warm blanket over her and giving her a kiss on her forehead.

Now, as she watched him, some of the last night's irritation slipped away. She also looked out the window to see the snow-covered mountains in the distance and the same white flakes on the ground from the day before. None of it had melted, and Ella was glad about that. She loved to just look at the snow. It was amazing to her, except for the hole she stepped in yesterday that it had covered.

At that thought, the pain in her foot seemed to come to life, though she was sure it was there before. At least her headache was gone, but it looked like she might need more medication after all, even though she didn't want to take it. She wanted to spend every minute with Seth that she could, and not in a drug-induced state. But they still had one thing they needed to straighten out: Tanner.

Tanner was a nice guy, Ella thought, but nothing compared to Seth. Why was Seth so insecure? Did he really think that she would just fall into another man's arms? Ella wasn't like that. In fact, she recalled the promise she had made to herself, that there was to be no significant other till she finished school, had a steady marketing job, and had a house of her own. She wanted to reach these goals before bringing someone into her life. But then she met Seth. It looked like destiny had other plans for her.

Seth's eyes opened sleepily. He appeared a bit disoriented, but she could understand, after all his travels over the last few days. As he stretched, she noticed the muscular body of this handsome man from top to toes. She smiled as she watched him because though she was physically attracted to him, for sure, it was his personality that she loved more. He was her Seth, that handsome, wouldn't-take-no-for-an-answer guy she met in Key West.

Usually, a persistent guy would get on her nerves, but not Seth. As she continued to watch him, Ella began to remember their time together in Key West. It had been a short three weeks, but something had started, and it involved Ella's heart. She only hoped that Seth felt the same way, though she still had to figure out the situation between the man she was staring at and his best friend.

"Good morning," Ella said before Seth could look over at her, but he quickly did so.

"Are you okay?" Seth asked, as though something was wrong.

"I'm fine, except I'm sorry I fell asleep so fast last night."

"No problem there. Those pain meds were a bit strong for you, but at least you seemed to be sleeping good before I passed out."

"Thanks for the blanket, and sorry I crashed on your couch."

"I'm sure your bed would have been more comfortable, but I didn't want to move you once you were comfortable. Wanted to make sure your foot stayed propped up to help the swelling. How are you feeling?" Seth asked.

"Okay. The headache is gone, but my foot is throbbing. Probably need some more medicine, but it makes me a bit loopy."

"Maybe we can call the doc today and see if there is something else you can take that isn't so strong."

"That sounds good."

Ella still felt a nervous energy from last night. They were both on edge. This isn't what she wanted when she decided to make this trip up here. So, it was time to clear the air this morning.

16

"Are you hungry?" Seth asked, not sure how to begin the morning. Last night had not gone as planned, but he wanted to make it up to her.

"A little, but I really need to shower and change clothes." She still had on the same outfit from yesterday. She hadn't wanted to try to take off the pants over her hurt foot, but now, she needed to.

"I don't mind helping you." As soon as the words were out of his mouth, Seth hoped that he didn't sound like he wanted more than to just help her. Though, he couldn't help but think of the possibilities, with the two of them alone in the house.

"Maybe if you could help me get upstairs and carry my clothes to the bathroom, I should be able to get it from there."

"I would be more than happy to help, and I'll stand outside the door, if you should need something."

"Then I'm ready whenever you are."

Ella swung her leg very carefully off the couch pillow it had been propped on all night and set the bandaged foot on the floor.

"Do you have a garbage bag and tape? I'm going to need to keep this covered while I'm in the shower."

"No problem." Seth quickly went to get both items, rummaging through a few drawers before he found the duct tape that would keep the bag securely around her foot. As he made his way back to the couch, Ella tried to get up by herself, but she wasn't as steady on her one good foot. But he was beside her to catch her just in time.

"You should have waited till I got back," Seth said, but being so close to her, it seemed like his words came out in a whisper.

"I thought that I could do it on my own, but I think I was mistaken."

Seth looked down on the beautiful woman he now held in his arms. This was different from when he had carried her yesterday. It was like a sense of electricity flowed from him to her and back again. He knew that she felt the same just by the look in her eyes.

"Ella, I'm really sorry about last night. Hell, everything yesterday."

"Why don't we talk about it after we get dressed? Maybe over some breakfast?"

"That sounds good." Seth felt a small chip in the ice that had surrounded their reunion thus far break, and it felt good.

Ella thought the same thing. Being with Seth right now, his arms wrapped around her in a protective embrace, was so different from yesterday. There was a tenderness there that made her heart melt. As she maneuvered on her crutches, he put one hand to the small of her back and his other arm out by her side, in case she needed help. Ella felt so protected and as though he would do anything to help her.

When they got to the steps, Ella decided the best way to tackle the steps would be by sitting on the step and scooting herself up, one step at a time. But before she could tell Seth her plan, he gently picked her up and took the steps slowly, watching her. It was like both of them were in a trance, watching the other silently, but so much was conveyed through their body language.

"Do you need help getting your clothes?" Seth stood awkwardly as he watched her rummage through her suitcase.

"I can pick them out, but if you could bring them to the bathroom, that would be a great help," Ella said. As she chose her outfit for the day, she knew that she could no longer wear the jeans she had just purchased. They wouldn't go over the bandage that tightly wound around her foot. What she did have were a pair of pajama bottoms, but they wouldn't keep her warm if they were to go anywhere.

Though Ella was thinking about her clothing situation, taking a shower and how she would maneuver herself around on one leg was more pressing on her mind. She would need help, but how could she ask Seth? Just his touch sent shivers through her. But to be naked in the same room? This was the most intimate thing they had encountered in their friendship so far, and Ella was already blushing at the thought.

"Everything okay?" Seth asked as Ella put her clothing in a pile with a cosmetic bag on top.

"Well, I don't have any pants that will go over this bandage on my foot, except for my pajamas. It will be too cold outside..." But Ella didn't get to finish her sentence.

"We aren't going anywhere today, so that's no problem."

"Nowhere? But I thought you wanted to show me the ranch? And what about dinner tonight, with Charlie and Mary?"

"The doctor said for you to rest."

Plus, Tanner showed you the ranch yesterday, Seth thought.

"I assumed that we could go riding or something like that," Ella said softly. "I'm feeling okay, except my foot is a little sore."

"A little sore?"

Ella couldn't hide the pain. She had already made the mistake of putting weight on her foot and let a small cry slip from her lips. "I know you're right, but I want to be outside."

"Let's take one thing at a time. Your shower first. How do you want me to help you?" Seth asked as he picked up the clothing Ella had chosen and then followed her to the bathroom.

"I guess if you don't mind turning around and just staying in the room? I think I can get undressed by myself. Maybe just be here in case I need something? I'm sorry to put you in this position."

"Really, it's no problem at all. I'm still sorry that you are even hurt. And that you can't fly back home when you were supposed to. I'm kind of glad you're stuck here with me a few extra days."

"What do you mean? I have to be back at work!"

Seth suddenly remembered that the doctor had told him and Tanner the details after Ella's accident, not Ella, since she had been given medicine.

"The doctor said he didn't think it would be a good idea for you to fly till sometime next week. He was worried about you making it through the airports by yourself, even though the staff would help you. But I told him we would handle the details when it was safe for you to travel."

"Seth, I'll lose my job. I was surprised they let me take time off, but I was persistent. Damn!"

Ella sat on the closed lid of the toilet, and a look of worry clouded her face.

"Maybe this wasn't such a good idea to come after all. So many mishaps. You. Me. Now, you and Tanner are upset at each other, like two teenage boys. Maybe this just isn't meant to be."

Seth felt all kinds of emotion coming to life inside of him, just hearing the words she spoke. Yes, everything had been more complicated than they anticipated, but he had never doubted that it would work out. Except he had reservations about Tanner's feelings for Ella, and vice versa.

Seth quickly came over and knelt down in front of Ella, lifting her chin to stare into the eyes that still mesmerized him.

"It'll be okay. I promise. Even if I have to drive you to Key West myself. And once your bosses hear about your accident, I'm sure they will understand."

"It'll be difficult being a waitress with a bum foot," Ella said, her voice filled with dejection.

"It will be fine." Seth reached over and kissed Ella on the cheek. He would have done more, but the situation and the room they were in didn't lend itself to a more intimate kiss.

"Right now, let's get you in the shower. I promise to keep my eyes closed as long as you promise to let me know if you need anything. Here are your clothes and everything you need to wrap up your foot." Seth placed the items on the bathroom sink.

"Okay. Let's see if I can do this." Ella reached and turned on the shower, then made her way back to the sink. True to his word, Seth had his back to her, and she stripped naked, sitting when she had to. She put the dirty clothes in a pile, neatly folded, then made her way to the shower. But then she realized that there was no way to get in without help.

"Seth?"

"What's wrong?"

"I need to step in the shower, but I don't think using my crutches would be such a good idea, and I don't feel like falling again. Think you might be able to keep your eyes closed and help me?"

All Seth could imagine was Ella standing naked not more than three feet from him, and it was difficult. How was he supposed to keep his wits about him when he would be touching her bare skin?

"No problem," Seth said, knowing the words he spoke were a lie. But he dutifully backed up till he felt Ella touch his back, the whole time keeping his eyes closed.

"All I need is to be able to lean on you just to get in the shower. Okay?"

"I'm right here."

Ella couldn't help but start laughing.

"What is it?"

"You just look so cute. You sure are squeezing your eyes shut so tightly."

"You don't know how tempting it is to open them."

"Thank you for being such a gentleman."

"If you knew what I was thinking, your opinion of me would change drastically."

Ella smiled at Seth, though he couldn't see her. "I appreciate everything you're doing for me. Just extend your arm out, and I'll use it to step in the shower."

Seth did as she instructed. As soon as he felt her hand on his forearm, the sizzle that went through his body was one that was hard to control. He felt Ella hop slightly, then heard her softly cry out.

"What's wrong?"

"Had to put a tiny bit of pressure on my foot, but I'm okay. This will be a quick shower, though."

Seth heard the shower door close. He was glad that it was a walk-in area, and there wasn't anything she had to step over. He heard her splashing in the water, and before he knew it, Seth opened his eyes, only looking forward, but it was the wrong thing to do. He forgot about the mirror on the back of the door, and it showed a very shapely Ella washing her hair. But fate must have known this would happen because the heat from the water had fogged up all the necessary places to keep Ella's body from being in full-view. But what he did see had Seth smiling widely. She was beautiful. Not just physically but in spirit as well. And that was why he had to make things right, then tell this woman how he truly felt.

"Seth, you're awfully quiet. Everything okay?" Ella said.

Seth found himself shutting his eyes quickly, as though he had been caught sneaking a peek. He hadn't meant to open his eyes, but he did. And what he saw would be forever etched in his memory.

"Everything is okay." And it was for Seth. He suddenly had the feeling that everything would be alright.

He heard the water turn off and the click of the shower door. "I'm right here, so just grab my arm if you need to." Seth stood there as he had at the beginning of the shower, arm extended. Suddenly, he felt her wet hand on his arm, and the same feeling he had before coursed through him yet again.

"I have my crutches now. Just give me a minute, and I'll be finished. I think I can do for myself from here."

"Then I'll be just outside, in the hall, if you need help."

Ella watched Seth walk out and close the door behind him. She smiled as she stood there, water still dripping from her skin. She had to tell him that she was falling in love with him. The feeling was growing stronger each moment they were together.

17

"So, what do you want to do today?" Seth asked as he put a vegetable omelet on Ella's plate, next to homemade potato fries.

"I didn't think you could cook," Ella said, looking at the plate before her.

"I never said I couldn't cook. Just that I usually didn't."

"Well, I want to go riding around. Look at the mountains closer. Ride on the horses. See the cattle closer. Maybe even drive that snowmobile."

Seth laughed. "I don't think any of that actually falls into what the doctor ordered. Remember, these need to be inside activities." As soon as the words left his mouth, Seth's imagination went into high gear with ideas of how he wanted to spend this time with Ella.

"I know. Just telling you what I would like to do. But you made me a promise that I would like to discuss."

"What are you talking about?" Seth asked, sitting beside her with his own plate.

"Are you going to fix things between you and Tanner?"

Seth paused just as he set his plate near hers on the table. He tried to figure out the best way to explain what was going through his head.

"I think Tanner likes you."

"I hope so. He's really nice. I would hate for your friends not to like me," Ella said.

"Not that kind of 'like'," Seth said, glancing at her sideways. Her eyes opened wide.

"Oh, I don't think so," Ella said, then paused. "Wait a minute. I thought you were thinking that I was interested in Tanner. It was him you were concerned about?"

"Ella, I confronted him when you were being looked at by the doctor. I asked him point-blank if he had feelings for you, and he didn't answer. That was all I needed to know."

Ella didn't know what to say. She had never done anything to lead Tanner on. "But that's silly! I've only been here three days. There is no way. He's charming, Seth, but he's not you. I don't think I did anything for him to think I was interested in him." Ella reached over and took Seth's hand. "This trip was to see you. Spend time with you and see where you live."

"I understand why he could feel something for you in such a short amount of time," Seth said softly, his food getting cold. "I was mesmerized by you on the first day we met."

Ella was speechless for the first time since she had arrived in town. Seth looked at her with his soft brown eyes, and her heart began to melt.

"I just have to tell you something."

"Tell me what?" Ella asked.

"Since I've been back home from that first trip to Key West, you have been constantly on my mind. For the first time since coming here to the ranch, I've actually thought about moving."

"Moving where?" Ella voice was almost a whisper, but Seth heard her loud and clear.

"The Keys. Because that's where you are."

"Are you serious? You'd do that?"

"In a heartbeat. Especially now that I've seen you again. Ella, I'm in love with you."

Ella's fork clinked her plate as it slid from her fingers. She was shocked at his declaration of love, but it only confirmed her feelings for him. She hadn't traveled all the way from south Florida just to see Montana. There was more to this trip than just to visit a friend.

"You love me?"

"I'm sorry. I know it's soon, but so much has happened these last few days that just confirmed everything I already knew. And I hate to say this, but when I looked out the window yesterday and saw you curled up in Tanner's arms, I wanted that to be me. I didn't know you were hurt at the time, but I wanted it to be me."

"I wanted it to be you too. When I got here and you weren't here, I was a bit disappointed. No, I was a lot disappointed. The surprise was ruined, but I realized that wasn't what had me sad. It was because the man I had fallen in love with wasn't here. I love you too, Seth. I don't believe in such things as a certain time frame where feelings are concerned. I think you just know when you know."

"So, you really don't like Tanner?" Seth smiled at her, causing Ella to laugh, but it didn't last long. He leaned over, and before she could say another word, he kissed her so deeply and with so much passion, it was like they melded into one.

"I hope that proved that I don't like Tanner. Well, I like him as a friend, but I love you, Seth Garner. I love you."

The next kiss was more intense than the first, and neither Seth nor Ella heard the knock at the door or the person coming into the house. But as Tanner came through the entryway and saw the couple in a heated embrace, he couldn't help but feel a little wave of sadness flow through him.

He knew Ella would never be someone for him, but she had given him hope that there was someone out there just for him. He had always flitted from one woman to another. But watching the scene before him, and after spending the last two days with Ella, Tanner knew he wanted more from a relationship than a one-night stand. He had Ella to thank for that. Now, if only he and Seth could repair their friendship, even though Tanner knew that he had done nothing wrong.

Tanner cleared his throat, catching the attention of both Ella and Seth. They turned quickly to see him standing there, both of them with a look of embarrassment on their faces.

"I promise I knocked, and when no one answered, I found the door unlocked and came in. Hope you don't mind."

"No, it's okay. That's how we are around the ranch," Seth said, not moving from Ella's side.

"Came by to let you know that we are going to be working on a pipe that busted last night. Plus, Mom wanted me to make sure that the two of you were coming to dinner tonight. She said that if Ella couldn't come, then she would be bringing dinner over here," Tanner said, very uncomfortable.

"I think we should be able to come," Ella said cheerfully. "Tanner, come join us for breakfast. Seth did the cooking."

"He did? Then I think I'll skip the invite," Tanner said with a smile.

"It's pretty good. And as far as for tonight, dinner sounds lovely. I should be able to hop my way over there with a little help." Ella looked up at Seth, who was standing beside her chair.

"Dinner sounds good, but we'll see how you feel tonight," Seth said, still not taking his eyes off Tanner. "So, a pipe burst?"

"Yeah, but it should be fixed soon."

"I want to go over a few more things. Let me walk you outside," Seth said. He leaned down to give Ella a kiss on the forehead, then headed toward Tanner. Then the two of them walked through the front door.

"Seth, sorry about walking in like that. I'm just used to how things are usually around here."

"It's okay. I probably would have done the same thing. In fact, I think I have a couple of times." Seth started laughing, and Tanner couldn't help but join him.

"Tanner, I owe you an apology. I had no right to blow up at you. I know that you wouldn't have done anything with Ella. I promise I do trust you. Just seeing you together made me realize a few things about Ella that I hadn't admitted to myself."

"Like you might be in love with the girl?" Tanner asked.

Seth smiled. They were best friends, and Tanner could read him like a book by now. But that also meant that Seth could do the same thing when it came to Tanner.

"You're right. She has certainly gotten under my skin, and I want to keep her by me. But I knew you had feelings for her too."

Tanner looked at the mountains in the distance, then back to his friend. "I'll admit that when I first saw her and spent some time with her, I was infatuated. And the thought did cross my mind that if she was here to visit you as just a friend, I was going to do everything I could to impress her. But she came here for you. The way she talked about you, the look in her eyes when I told her about things we had done together over the years, I could see she only had feelings for you. So, I want you to know that you are one damn lucky guy. Anyone would love to have a woman like Ella, so you better be good to her. If not, you'll have to answer to me."

Seth hugged his friend. This is what he wanted to hear and to know.

"There is someone out there for you, Tanner."

"Maybe I need to go to Key West. It seemed to work for you."

"Well, I will say that it is mighty nice down there, and the women are pretty hot."

"So, we'll see you two tonight, then?'

"As long as Ella's foot isn't any worse. She wants to go horseback riding, back out to look at the cattle, and go the mountains."

"Didn't the doc say for her to rest today?"

"You spent a few days with her. Do you think she is one to follow doctor's orders?"

"You're right there. Then all I can say is good luck, and we'll see you tonight. Either at Momma's and Daddy's house or over here. Tell Ella I said 'bye'."

"Will do." Seth watched as Tanner's truck pulled out of the driveway and down the road. Things felt right again and even better knowing that Ella loved him.

Now, to find a way to make her stay off that foot, Seth thought to himself as he went back into the house.

"Tanner gone?" Ella asked.

Seth saw that she had eaten every bit of food on her plate.

"Sorry. I tried to wait, but I was really hungry."

Seth could only smile. "I'm just glad you liked it. It's been a while since I cooked."

"Then we will have to make sure we cook a few more times. I think cooking together could be fun. Plus, I find it quite sexy to see a man in the kitchen."

"You do?" Seth now had her wrapped in his arms.

"Most definitely. So, what are we doing today?" Ella's eyes looked excited, but Seth sensed the pain in them too.

"Today is what we here at the ranch call movie day."

"Movie day?"

"Yes. I'm going to get some more firewood and make sure we have a nice fire going. We have all the makings for, well, just about everything since you went to the store. And we are going to just spend some time together, watching movies, eating, and maybe even a nap. Plus, you, my dear, are going to keep that foot propped up and take your medicine."

Ella's face was now sporting a frown.

"I know you want to go places, and believe me, I want to show you around and do all kinds of things. But we will have more time for that later."

"But I have to leave in a few days."

"That's if the doctor clears you to go anywhere."

"Even with that, I'll be leaving shortly."

"Then since we have all day to hang around the house, why don't we talk about a few things."

"Like what?"

"About me and you." Seth leaned in once again, taking Ella's lips and kissing them fully, leaving both of them a little breathless.

18

"What is this?" Seth asked. He held out what seemed to be an old sweatshirt, with several holes in various places, and looked over at Ella.

"What does it look like? A sweatshirt!"

"Okay, I know that, but is it yours? I mean, I can't imagine you wearing this down here."

"I've had that since I was a little girl," Ella said, taking the special vase that was in her hands and carefully wrapping it in newspaper.

"Is it going with you?"

"Of course! I even still sleep in it occasionally." Ella smiled with mischievous eyes.

"You know, there are things you can sleep with that make things more comfortable."

"And you have a suggestion, I imagine."

"Yes, I can think of one," Seth said, coming up behind Ella. He kissed her on her neck as she placed two more items in the box and sealed the lid.

"I think I know who you're thinking about, and if I'm right, I couldn't agree with you more." Ella turned her body in Seth's arms, so she was now facing him. She laid her head against his chest and wrapped her arms around his waist. It felt so good to be in his arms, this close, almost like one person.

"Are you sure this is what you want to do?" Seth asked, laying his head against hers.

"I've never been more sure in my life."

"And your parents are okay with it?"

"I can't say they are thrilled, but they know I'm a grown woman and can make my own choices. When I left Miami, I think they had doubts if I could make it on my own. But I did it. So, now, they don't question me as much. They even liked you!"

Seth remembered that night. He was so nervous, knowing that he was meeting Ella's parents and the stories she had told him about her upbringing. Ella had described them as so strict that he wasn't sure what to expect. And even though they had only spent one evening together, everything had gone perfectly. Seth could tell that Ella's parents, especially her dad, had lots of questions about what they had planned to do, but he had nothing but praise for his daughter.

Mr. Cummings had spoken with Seth privately and told him in no uncertain terms to take care of his daughter, or he would answer to him. Seth respectfully told him that Ella meant everything to him and that he would not do anything to hurt her. The two men shook hands, and it was as though Seth had a seal of acceptance from Ella's family. That had meant more to him than he could say.

Seth's father, Michael, and stepmother, Josie, had even been there for the meal that evening, and everyone had gotten along so well that it seemed like this group had done this many times over the years. It was a shame that almost three thousand miles would be separating them now, but Ella assured her parents that she was only a plane ride away and that they were going to love visiting her and Seth in Montana.

"Are you sure you want to move away from all this?" Seth said as they walked along Duval Street, toward Mallory Square to watch the Sunset Celebration.

Ella looked around and then back at Seth. "More than sure. I can't say I won't miss it, and I hope that we can own a house here that we can come and visit as much as possible. But my place is with you. I know that now more than ever."

The rest of Ella's trip to Montana had gone off without a hitch. She had spent two days resting, making sure her foot was okay. As soon as the swelling was down and she could put a small amount of weight on the foot with the help of a walking boot, she and Seth had explored the area around the ranch. And with each place they went, Ella fell in love. More deeply with Seth, but also with Montana.

Ella had never imagined living anywhere else besides a place where the daily attire was tank tops, shorts, and flip-flops, but Montana had seeped into her soul. The crisp mountain air, the snow, and even the colder temperatures appealed to her, except she seemed to be wearing more clothes than anyone else she saw. Everyone even kidded her about having to wear three pair of socks just to keep her feet warm.

But Ella didn't care. It was beautiful there, and she wanted this next adventure in her life to include Seth and his world. They had made plans to visit his mom in Seattle, and Ella couldn't wait to explore more of the Northwest. She even hoped that they would go to California and on to see the Southwest deserts. Seth promised that they would do that and more when she finished her degree. It was to be her graduation gift, and that was only a month away.

This probably wasn't the best time to make a major move, but she didn't want to be away from Seth any more than she had already. Their crazy, mixed-up trip had solidified their feelings for each other, and they were ready to take their relationship to the next level.

They reached the Square, and everything was in full-swing. There were people everywhere, and Ella loved every minute of it. A tear came to her eye because she knew that she would miss this, but it also gave her something to looked forward to when they visited.

Seth had her hand in his, and they wound their way through the people to find a seat along the pier to watch the sunset. But just as they both sat down, Seth quickly stood back up, jumping up on a little step beside Ella.

"Hello, everyone," Seth yelled to the crowd immediately surrounding them. "Can I have your attention?"

Ella looked at him as though he had lost his mind. What in the world was he doing?

The people around them were now staring at him, trying to figure out what this man was going to do. And then Seth began.

"You see this woman right here?" Seth pointed to Ella, and he took her hand, pulling her up to her feet. "We met not too far from here and not too long ago. But you know what? I'm so in love with this woman that I don't know how to put it into words, so I hope this will do."

Seth jumped down, still in front of Ella, then bent down on one knee. Ella was shocked as she watched him and then looked around to see a large crowd surrounding them.

"Ella, would you do me the most wonderful honor of becoming my wife?"

Ella stood there, dumbfounded. She was speechless. As she glanced around, she saw that everyone was waiting for her answer. But none looked as nervous as Seth as he peered up at her.

"What do you say? Let's make this a permanent thing before we leave here tomorrow."

"You mean get married?" Ella exclaimed.

"Right now, I'll just accept a 'yes' to being my wife."

"Well, good because I can imagine a wedding in Montana in the summer."

"So, is that a 'yes'?" Seth asked, coming to stand upright in front of her.

"Most definitely!"

Ella practically flung herself into Seth's arms, and the crowd around them cheered. It was as though they had been watching a street performance, and everyone began shaking their hands, wishing them luck. A few people that had just a bit too much to drink gave elaborate toasts in their honor.

As the crowd settled down, Ella and Seth took their places back on the pier. Ella snuggled back against Seth, and he held her closer. Ella couldn't quit looking at the large sparkling ring Seth had placed on her finger and then back at the sun as it settled below the horizon.

This had been one of the best nights of her life. And tomorrow, she was starting on another journey. The van was packed with her things, and she and Seth were driving back to Montana. A new adventure, and one she couldn't wait to begin.

"I love you so much, Seth. The last trip might have been a big mix-up, but it led to some wonderful things."

"I couldn't agree more, future Mrs. Garner."

"I like that sound of that," Ella said, then gently kissed him on the lips. "I love you."

"I love you too, Ella. Are you ready for Montana?"

"As long as you are there with me, I'm ready for anything."

Acknowledgements

So I said there would be no more "Florida Keys Novels" but I never said I wouldn't write a novella! And this story was so much fun to write.

Each "Florida Keys Novel" I wrote was filled with lots of minor characters that I'm sure I could write full length novels about but I love the idea of small novellas. Think of them as extended short stories.

I was really excited to tell a very small portion Seth and Ella's story. Truthfully, Seth didn't come into the picture for a while but from the moment I wrote of Abbey's next-door neighbor, Ella, I knew she had a story to tell. Though this is only a fraction of her story, MAYBE one day, I might just have to expand the story. We shall see.

But I have many people to thank for the encouragement they gave me along the way to enable me to take these characters and tell their story too. I know that each time I write this part of the book, it is either my mom or my husband that get top credit but this time I can't choose. My mom, Irene, has been so instrumental in helping me sort out ideas, listening to me talk endlessly about story lines and then reading my novels over and over, helping me to get them just right.

Then on the other hand, I have my wonderful husband, Jeff that is my rock. He gives me the space and time to write these stories that circle around in my head. From taking care of our pup, Emma, to washing clothes, fixing dinner and just about anything else I need, he is right there, always supporting me. I really can't thank my husband or my mom enough for their endless support of my dream to write.

My dad, Sonny, has been a sounding board for me as I tackle the business side of this author world. It can sometimes feel daunting but in reality it is just another learning experience. I want to thank him so much for the guidance and wisdom he has shared and continues to do so with each decision I make on this journey.

To my editor and publisher – thanks for your patience and the endless questions I still have even after writing ten books. It seems like this business is ever changing and probably always will be. But life is like that so I shouldn't be surprised. I'm just lucky enough to have so many people around me that support me, help me and listen to me, especially when I'm trying to find my way.

To all my new author friends and the best selling authors that continue to inspire me – thank you so much for what you do. Watching as you continue to write one book after another, to much success, gives me people to look up to and strive for excellence as you have.

With much love to all,

Miki

Other Novels By Miki Bennett

"The Florida Keys Novels" series
The Keys to Love
Forever in the Keys
Run Away to the Keys
Back to the Keys
A Wedding in the Keys
A Folly Beach Christmas novella

"Camping in High Heels" series
Camping in High Heels
Camping in High Heels: Las Vegas
Camping in High Heels: California
Camping in High Heels: Yellowstone

"The Nauterian Novels"
She Came from the Sea

Other Books
You in a Book series

About The Author

Miki Bennett is the best-selling author of the *Florida Keys Novels, Camping in High Heels series* and *The Nauterian Novels*. She is also of the author of a book about journaling - *You in a Book*. When she's not writing, Miki enjoys going to the beach, spending time outdoors, and doing crafts. She lives in Charleston, South Carolina, with her husband, Jeff and little dog, Emma.

www.ingramcontent.com/pod-product-compliance
Lightning Source LLC
Chambersburg PA
CBHW070334130626
46556CB00007B/2850